Game of Lies: Hidden Truth

Sometimes we grow up thinking that our family is going to stick together because we share the same blood. Never knowing which way life will take us or how our children will end up. From friendships to brotherhood nothing is never too close to be tested in life! But only God can determine who our real family is, but we are not God to determine who our real family will be.

When Shantelle thought she had it all nothing that Jordan was doing was wrong the love of her life was the perfect match to her life. Wait until Shantelle finds out that in a blink of an eye her whole world can change in a split second. Independence and Self-love is everything; Shantelle finds out this the hard way. Meet the Dunkin family Shantelle and Jordan Dunkin. A middle class couple from Pikesville Maryland living in a condo off Reisterstown Road. The condo has a private entrance and a security code on everything so what would Shantelle ever had to worry about? Nothing at all she has everything a 36-year-old mother of twin girls could ever want. Shantelle never thought that her world could change by the family secrets coming out one by one. Always playing it cool Shantelle never thought that her husband Jordan would play himself out of position. Shantelle wants the world to see all the good in her marriage and not face the reality that her perfect world might be affected by a short storm. The plot will thicken, the tea be stirred and it gets hot in this story. Shantelle and Jordan Dunkin will see the storm brewing but who will survive?

Game of Lies:Hidden Truth

Chapter 1

There is always love

Marrying the man of her dreams Mr. Jordan Dunkin her first true love they have been together from the classrooms of Douglas High to the streets of Popular Grove. Shantelle knew Jordan's every move, his every little secret; she was like one of the guys. That night he asked her to marry him was nothing shear of romance as Jordan was quite the hopeless romantic thug. Jordan would hold Shantelle when she would run to him after leaving home from a fight with her mom and step dad. Growing up a fatherless child and not too sure what real love felt like Shantelle always would turn to Jordan for the comfort her family never gave her. That night that Shantelle told Jordan that for the past ten years her step father was touching her in her sleep." I have missed my period Jordan." Shantelle tells Jordan with real tears falling and fear in her voice. Knowing that the baby was her step fathers Shantelle tells Jordan everything from the nights that he would rape her to the days when she would catch him standing over her jerking his penis over top of her while she was asleep. "How am I going to tell my mother that her husband got me pregnant Jordan?" Shantelle asked. "Your not going to get an abortion and we're not going to tell a soul. I am going to pay for it and get Cynthia to go with you. That's what real friends do for each other babe." Jordan explained.

Sitting in the back of Jordan's '99 Lexus ES 300 Shantelle falls asleep in his arms crying thinking that her life is over. Jordan holds Shantelle tight and whispers, "Let me handle this Shanny for you I got this, I will take care of everything." Wiping her tears he then kisses her forehead and they climb in the front seat as Jordan takes Shantelle home for the night. "Go in there baby and act normal if anything pops off tonight hit my pager." Jordan says as he says his goodnights to Shantelle. Walking into her mother's house Shantelle speaks to her step-father and mother and says her good nights and then heads to her room. Her little sister Taylor always follows her to the room when she sees Shantelle going to bed. Their bonds were so tight nothing could break them especially since their older sister Crystal has been moved out after having a fight with her mother and step-father. Shantelle laid in her bed and let the tears fall that night as Taylor laid there and played in her hair. Caressing her curls as she cries herself to sleep Taylor whispered to her sister. "One day Shanny just one day he will pay for this. He will not hurt you anymore I promise you." Wiping her face Shantelle looks up at her baby sister and says, "No no he won't once I get rid of this baby I am going to get rid of his ass." Looking at her in shock Taylor couldn't even get her words out without starting to cry," Your pregnant by John! Does Mom know?" "She can never know Tay NEVER!", Shantelle responds.

May 17,1997 Senior prom is here Jordan is on time; sharp as a tack waiting for Shantelle to come down the steps in her gold floor length dress. Standing outside in his '99 Lexus nice and clean Jordan opens the door for Shantelle like the perfect gentleman that his mother raised him to be. "Oh my God you are beyond perfect Shantelle." Jordan says as she walks out the house and steps into the car. That night was nothing short of amazing for both Jordan and Shantelle. Waking up in a hotel room in VA still fully clothed and in Jordan's arms; Shantelle knew from that night forward he was way more than her best friend but he was her true first love. Graduation day Shantelle thought that was going to be the day that her secret hit the fan after the fight her parents had the night before. Shantelle heard her mother fussing about how her step father never spends time alone with her and how he always out in the streets. And then the shit hit the fan "So tell me who you been fucking John?" Shantelle's mother asked. It took everything in her to hold her tongue and not to yell out that he would sneak in her room at night while her mom was sleeping and fuck her and how dare he get her pregnant. Shantelle laid in her bed thinking not too much longer she would be on a college campus and living a real private life. Walking across that stage at the Baltimore arena hearing her name being called to receive her diploma (with tears falling) the tears fall. Shantelle said to herself I made it.

The summer was nothing but work, laid back fun and hanging with Jordan and his boys. Anything from watching them play ball to shopping at the mall for the latest party outfits. Shantelle and Cynthia had become inseparable during the summer everywhere that Shantelle was you saw Cynthia. Watching their bond grow Jordan was happy that Shantelle found someone to talk to; there is nothing like a close friend. Driving up 695 to White Marsh Mall Cynthia sparks a conversation, "Shanny you got everything you need for Coppin?" "Naw I still need to go over there this week and sign the papers for my dorm but God knows I can't wait to get the hell out of my parent's crazy ass house." Shantelle replies. Talking about college and getting everything that they need for the new college life Shantelle and Cynthia seem to find that they have so much in common.

I can't believe that this day has come the day that my baby is leaving home to go off to the college dorm. Shantelle's mother cries as she watches her baby girl walk onto the campus of Coppin State College. Watching her mother cry tears of joy Shantelle cried tears of relief. The fact that she was free from the hands of John no more being touched by him at night while she slept. Thinking this will be one of the best decisions she made in her life. Shantelle walked in the dorm and low and behold she meets her roommate Dawn. Dawn was Shantelle's best friend from middle school who moved to Howard County in the 8th grade. The two laughed, jumped ,cried then they laughed some more. Sitting on the bed catching up Shantelle was telling Dawn about Jordan her homeboy as she described him. Dawn caught Shantelle up on what happen when she was in the 8th grade and why she moved. Dawn had a little baby girl when she was 14. She was raped by the man who lived on their street was how Dawn described the baby she had by Shantelle's step-father John. Listening to Dawn tell her story Shantelle felt the tears fall as she started to share with Dawn that she too; had been raped and impregnated by her own step-father. The ladies shared so many stories that night they never left the dorm room or had dinner.

With classes day in and day out, Shantelle found an escape from the pain she carried from her past. Never going to bed at night without a meal with Jordan and a good night text to follow Shantelle always smiled; Without…Never crossing the line and having sex Shantelle felt that one day that day would eventually come for her and Jordan. He seemed to miss hanging with her so Jordan tried his best to keep her smiling. Six years of books, stepping with the squad in her sorority Shantelle was ready for that step with her best friend Dawn right beside her. Dawn and Shantelle had made so many plans for after college. Shantelle was in her room getting dressed for graduation and then she hears Taylors voice calling her into the living room. Shantelle rushes out to see that Jordan has had 20 dozen of red and pink roses and a teddy bear with her name on it and a cap and gown that read "To My Shining Star" on it. Helping her big sister get ready for her graduation, Taylor started telling Shantelle that she is moving to California in six months. She has applied for a dance school that takes high school seniors and gets them into the lights of Hollywood.

Dinner and dancing was fun something different for Shantelle, Dawn showed Shantelle fun outside the city from horse riding to the gun range. Shantelle and Dawn started spending so much time together that Cynthia had become very jealous of their friendship. Watching the two get ready for Dawn's mother's sixtieth birthday party Cynthia asked Shantelle, "So tell me what has been up with you lately? I haven't talked to you or been able to spend any real time with you." "I really didn't think that you would want to do the things that Dawn and I like to do." Shantelle replied. Finishing getting dressed before Jordan came Shantelle tells the ladies to hurry Jordan will be there by 8 and it was 7:45 already. Not thinking that Cynthia was really that jealous of their relationship Shantelle ignored her attitude. On their way to the party Jordan stops the car in the middle of Campfield Road it's all dark and the girls are all looking at him like he was crazy. Jordan pulls the car over and walks over to Shantelle's door, opens it her door and kneels down asking her to become his wife. Shantelle thought that is was a joke so she laughed until Jordan pulls out this 5 carat white gold diamond ring and engraved on the left side of the band is his name. Tears fall from Shantelle's facee and as she says yes.

Shantelle spent every day on the computer looking for the perfect dress, shoes, and venue the perfect shoe, the perfect Venue. Shantelle decided to try to reach out to one of her classmates who she remembered that used to play around with her camera in college to see if she could can take pictures of her and Jordan for their engagement. Wedding planning is fun for Shantelle as her and Jordan sit down day by day picking out things for their wedding and their new house. Jordan decided that he will not take his future wife into an apartment instead he decided to purchase a brand new home for him and his wife. A nice four bedroom Cape Cod in Pikesville in a nice gated community with a garage and a parking pad all set for a family that they talked about planning of over the past few months. Shantelle decided that she was going to have to hire decorators to come in and complete the house prior to the wedding and the move in.

The night before the wedding Shantelle sat in Taylor's room talking to her about their future. Taylor was so excited that her big sister was not only getting out of the ghetto but getting from up under John and her mother's roof. Shantelle was teaching Taylor how to bank and how to save money for her future endeavors. Not realizing that she had been up all night out of excitement Shantelle gets ready for her big day. It is here and she is so elated! Shantelle is excited that it is time for the bridal prep. All the girls have arrived and they are ready for the primping and pampering moment before the tears, and the cheers. Dressing the bride all of the bridal party is accounted for, a soft knock on the door is heard. Wondering who that could be Taylor opens the door to the bell man at the hotel and he is holding gift boxes all named for each woman in the wedding party and one big box addressed to Shantelle. Opening the boxes Jordan has brought each woman a diamond bracelet from Tiffany's with a thank you message engraved on the inside of each bracelet. The cards are all marked "These are to be worn today", signed the king to the best queen to be. Opening her box Shantelle notices that she has a single rose attached to a card that read "If every pedal and every stem was a way to your heart I would take every flower from every garden." A Diamond bracelet and pendant to match her that matched that 5 carat diamond ring and the pendant to match made for great accessories for Shantelle's wedding dress.

The wedding and honeymoon is over the pictures are back and are hung high in the house. The mornings are normal Shantelle gets up and cooks breakfast and starts her day while as Jordan has always done his morning run (just a suggestion: to the reservoir and back home run and then back home. Today was a little different though today Jordan let her sleep in as he took his morning run. Rolling over Shantelle felt that something wasn't right her morning was thrown off by an acute illness she has been experiencing every day. Looks like mommy need that extra rest today because she is very tired and ill. Allowing his pregnant wife to sleep in Jordan starts his day as normal his morning run then back home to his loving wife then off to work. Shantelle was working from home for her marketing company because she was on bedrest carrying with her twins. Not able to eat much she rested for hours on end. While getting the nursery together Jordan and Shantelle shopped for everything the well-loved twins could possibly need. The day has finally come 2 beautiful 6 lb. baby girls for Shantelle and Jordan. No more sleeping at night for the loving newlyweds. Jordan is back to work a week after the twins are born. Dawn and Cynthia take turns helping Shantelle with the babies while Jordan works during the day. The Dunkin family seems to be complete.

Chapter 2

Out like a light

For the first time in over 10 months Shantelle gets a chance to hang out with her friends she was so happy to leave the kids and get fresh air. Walking out the house dressed in her tight skirt to show off her phat ass Shantelle was ready for the bar that night. With a crop top on to show off her full figure those twins gave her Shantelle was on fire. Jordan was left behind with the babies and his homeboys. Trying to get things in order Jordan had the babies in the family room with him and Pun his best friend of 20 years or more. Jordan and Pun have been friends since they were in elementary school. Sitting in the Livingroom rapping about the past Jordan reflects with Pun on a time when his mother brought home his little brother from the hospital and she was in so much awe because she had a new baby on Christmas day. Yo! My mother kept saying "This is the best Christmas gift I ever received, Thank you Sr. for my gift." Jordan said to Pun. "Funny was the Disney trip in '90 when we went with you and your parents and we had so much fun yo, my mother was so broke she sent us with underwear only. I was so heated with her when we left our house your father had taken all of us to the mall and got us shoes and clothes for the trip." Pun said. "Our Families were so close when we were growing up and we were even closer that's why we 'are brothers no matter what!" Jordan said. The two sat and watched the basketball game and talked and smoked Pun asked Jordan about his night club he had open about a year ago. "Yo, I still haven't been down to Jordi's since the opening night. You know that the streets are always busy how is business going at the club? I heard you got new chicks up in there since the last time I came in through. There last? I was thinking of coming down this weekend. " Yo, business is booming and the girls are fire in there Yo, between you and I do you remember lil Ana from Cherry Hill she up in there on Thursdays bar tending I saw she wasn't working so I gave her a bar tending gig. Jordan said. "Anastasia? That is my little sister Yo nobody never knew that she was my sister because we were so far apart and she was always in Cherry Hill with my aunt and her father's family so she was never home but Yo that's my sister Yo! Pun replied. "WOW Baltimore is small as shit Yo!" Jordan said. They continued to watch the game and smoke until the girls woke up and then Shantelle would be home before too long.

Jordan started to think back to how things were when his mother was around him and how his brother took her for granted for so long. Jordan was never the mama's boy he always would follow behind his father watching his father go from this woman's house to that woman's house selling those women drugs and fucking them. Jordan had saw so much hanging with his father for so many years but never said anything to his mother about what his father was out there doing. For so long he always thought that his father was sleeping with the lady down the street Ms. Alex not to mention she was Pun's mother too. He would watch his father go in the house and be in there for about an hour while he played outside. Until that one day he asked his father "What do you and Ms., Alex be in there doing daddy?" His father looked at him and said "Adult shit son adult shit." Thinking that he was just fucking every woman in the city Jordan swore that he would never be like his father and that he would be so much better then him when he grew up. Watching his mother suffer for years sleeping alone at night crying because there was no food in the house and his father was out there in the streets but he would always bring home money for the bills but would think that the food stamps that my mother received would feed us and it was never enough. I hated my life Jordan thought I want to be so much better for my family I vowel to that shit. Praying to the Lord that he would be such a better person for his family he asked God to cover him as a man, n and a father and, a husband to not be anything like his father.

Having a ball at the lounge with Cynthia and Dawn, Shantelle had drank so much she couldn't believe that she was even drinking that much. Shantelle was ready to go home about an hour in to being out with her girls. She just didn't say anything to her friends because she didn't want to be a party pooper. Rushing to the bathroom to throw up after drinking so much Shantelle really was ready to go at that point. Dawn and Cynthia helped her into the house and up to her room as they saw that Jordan and the twins were knocked out in the family room and Pun was gone. Not waking a soul they put Shantelle to bed and then snuck out the house. Running from the bed to the toilet Shantelle couldn't seem to get it together after drinking. Jordan heard his wife upstairs throwing up so he went to aide her as the babies were still asleep in their beds. Cleaning her up and getting her back in the bed Jordan holds his wife as she suffers for the night.

Waking the next morning thinking that she was about to die the night before Shantelle couldn't feel her face or her feet; and she couldn't make it out of bed. Jordan was sitting on the end of the bed laughing at how his wife looked in the morning after drinking. Changing up his routine for a day to nurse cater to his wife, Jordan

catered to Shantelle hand and foot. Rubbing her feet and caressing her back and

rubbing every inch of her body. Jordan began to kiss on Shantelle's back and then one

thing led to another; next thing you know Jordan had his head between Shantelle's legs

licking her in every spot that made her squirm. Making love to each other there's

nothing like when they climax together Shantelle feels so connected to Jordan. Jumping

in the shower Shantelle felt a little better she made her way down to the family rooms

with the twins and called Dawn to see if she was coming over to spend time with her

god daughters. Dawn's phone kept going to voicemail, so Shantelle left a message on

her voicemail for her to call her when she got up.

Time goes by nothing seems to be out of place, but Shantelle wasn't

feeling herself she couldn't figure out what was wrong with her. She was always sleepy

and always feeling sick. Shantelle went down to the kitchen to see if Jordan was down

there. Calling Cynthia and then Dawn on a conference call Shantelle tells them her

news. "Girls I'm pregnant AGAIN!! Jordan is going to be so happy he is going to think

that he is going to be a father of a baby boy. The girls were so happy they decided to try

to play a trick on Jordan and place little hints around the house and see if he could

figure out what was going on. After his morning run Jordan comes in the house and he

sees the first hint on the kitchen table a baby sock with a tag that said "oh my." Not

thinking anything of it Jordan makes his way to the shower where he always go straight

after a morning run. The next clue was there a bottle of baby bath. Still not thinking

anything of it Shantelle is sitting in the room laughing as Jordan comes into the room

gives her kisses and says his good mornings. Reaching over to kiss the babies on the bed Jordan notices that they are not dressed alike this is a real first he then says "what is going on Babe something feels different." Shantelle laughs and says "nothing, get yourself ready for work Bae I know you have a long day ahead of you. " Opening the closet door Jordan notices a receipt from Rite-Aid for a pregnancy test. Jumping up and down Jordan says "Oh my we are having another baby." With pure excitement they celebrate the pregnancy.

Making plans for the new baby that is coming Shantelle and Jordan begin to get things in order for the growing family. A knock at the door wondering who it could be Shantelle opens the front door and it's the UPS man with boxes from Tiffany's and Louis Vuitton all addressed to her. Jordan always surprised her with small gifts until she had the twins then he started giving her bigger gifts. Shantelle pulled out the bracelet engraved with the girls name on it and then she opened the other box and pulled out her matching bags; a diaper bag and matching monogram LV bag. Smiling from ear to ear she runs into the room with Jordan and kisses and hugs him with thanks.

With the painters leaving and the room all together to welcome their third daughter Shantelle Jordan and the twins settle down for the night, by watching a movie in the family room. Falling asleep in Jordan's arms Shantelle is in her zone she always feels so safe when she is with him. Jumping up from a nightmare Shantelle realizes that her water has broken she wakes Jordan and they hurry rush to the hospital. Rushing through the doors of labor and delivery at Sinai hospital Jordan calms Shantelle as she feels the need to push. Waiting on the doctor to come into the room the nurse preps Shantelle for delivery. The doctor notices that the baby heart rate is constantly dropping and Shantelle is not breathing right he rushes her in to get a C-section and he puts her on oxygen immediately. After the procedure the nurses rush the baby to the NICU. The baby is blue and she is she is blue and not responding her heart beat is faint and Shantelle is not coming to either. The doctors monitor Shantelle as she comes from under the anesthesia. Not sure how to break the terrible news to the parents that baby girl Dunkin didn't make it through the delivery, the Doctor calls Jordan into the hallway to explain. She didn't make it, because that the umbilical cord was wrapped around her neck and she lost her breathing during the delivery and did not make it through. Jordan broke down in the hallway and begged asked the doctors not to tell Shantelle yet that she died yet. Shantelle was still coming to when she saw Jordan crying she immediately began to cry and asked what was wrong before he could tell her she screamed "not my baby no!!!!" Not sure how to handle things Shantelle asked to see the baby she wanted to hold her and just kiss her a good night.

No day is ever the same in the Dunkin house Shantelle and Jordan is back to work and Jordan is working to the twins are in day care and everyone is going on with life. The nursery is still put together with no baby to put in the new crib or even to rock in the chair. Jordan went into the nursery and sat in the rocking chair and the tears began to fall, he Jordan was thinking about his mother and how the fact that his daughter was going to have her name and carry it well; and now both of them were gone. Jordan couldn't stop the tears from falling feeling like he had failed his wife and children kids because of the he lost of his new baby girl. Listening to Faith Evans sing I miss you Jordan thinks of baby Asia and yells out "Why GOD?! Why my baby?! She didn't even have a chance at life! Lord why must you take her from me?"

Game of Lies:Hidden Truth

A letter comes in the mail from the hospital for with a memorial planned for the baby. Debating on whether they want to go or not Shantelle and Jordan decide to go and honor their baby girl. Guiding his wife Jordan knows that he is going to be hurt from this but he must stay strong for Shantelle. They return from the service and try to finish going on with life not planning anything big or even planning another baby Shantelle and Jordan go to therapy to seek healing. Waking up plenty of nights with nightmares of having the baby and needing Jordan to wipe her tears Shantelle thought that she was falling apart nothing in her life has ever hurt this bad. This feeling was worse than when she found out she was pregnant and had to get rid of the baby. Jordan was that loving spirit that his family needed him to be. He never allowed his pains of losing his baby girl show through while in spending time with the twins or Shantelle. "No day will ever be the same in my heart I don't know why God is punishing me." Jordan cried while in the shower the next morning getting ready for his day. Life changed from that day on for Jordan and Shantelle they found focus in work and the twins doing family trips and family activities to keep busy.

Thinking about starting a new Job in the evening Shantelle talks things over with Jordan. She wants a change in the jobs, because between the stresses that she face after having the baby Shantelle cannot find focus at the firm she is working at right now. Jordan thinks that the new job may help them in saving money on day care as well. The twins are getting older and they are walking around the house. There are gates everywhere in the house to keep them out the kitchen and from going down the steps. Shantelle explained that the pay would be better and she would do anything to keep Jordan from going back in the streets. He has been lying low for ten years just so to keep his family together. Feeling like her past has brought her so far and with the

love of Jordan and him protecting their family Shantelle had her life in line for once.

Sitting in her room writing in her journal about where she has come from Shantelle

comes across a letter she received when she was in college from Jordan's mother

stating that she was leaving Jordan's father. She had caught him with another woman

and that she is not telling her children. Shantelle had forgotten all about her Mother in

law leaving her this letter before she killed herself in 2001. Jordan walked in on

Shantelle reading the letter and watched as the tears fell from her eyes.

Chapter 3

I Thought He would never Cheat!!!

Months has passed since that tragic day that the Dunkin's lost their baby girl. Shantelle lays in bed early Monday morning before dropping the girls at daycare at 8 looking over her life thinking. There is nothing like waking up every day knowingly thinking that you can conqueror the world. "Watching him get up on time with the same routine, with nothing changing from the way he showers to the way he brushes his teeth. It's 10 after nine time for his morning run then back by 10 for his morning shower. Then he hits the streets. No day is different in his world to you the routine and is the same the money never changes. He pays all the bills and fucks you like he misses you before work every day. Picks the kids up from school, helps them with their homework and has your bathe water ready every night after work. On to the night shift he goes. You trust his truth cause nothing ever seems to change the routine is the same. No drama from other bitches so he can't be entertaining anyone other than his wife. You never hear his name in the streets he wouldn't do that to you, he wouldn't have you thinking he's working when he is really entertaining another and another. That's my man we eat and live as a family. That's not nothing he plays about his family comes first. HE FUCKS ME RIGHT from flipping to kissing he has you all over the place in that bed making you cum time after time. He can't be sleeping around because he don't even bust fast. He makes love to you like never before each time its better and better. Telling you "um-mm you better not ever leave me, don't you ever give my pussy away." "It's your pussy daddy, I would never cheat!" But he never replies "neither would I" so is he out there? No not my man not the way he makes love to me and sends those chills

through my body. Umm! I love the way he feels the chemistry between us is everything

and I love it. OOOO…….. I love him and when he turns me over I cum so hard that's my

man he belongs right here where he is. BUT IS HE ALL MINES?" Shantelle recites her

last poetry entry to herself for her open mic night she signed up for with Dawn.

Nothing is different today same routine Jordan wakes up and runs same time

back home and showers. Same ole routine, fucks the shit out of me before work! "Oh

shit I came hard as fuck today" Why My Jordan fucks me really hard today what's

different, nothing guess it was that argument last night. So much has changed in our

lives in the past year I couldn't imagine my life without Jordan and my girls Shantelle

says to herself. The bell rings "good morning how may I help you?" Shantelle ask the

young man at the door, a man hands me court papers with Jordan Dunkin Jr. name on it

she read it and look through it "OH SHIT" she screams "Jordan has a paternity test

court date for next month. Who the fuck is this?!" Shantelle says to the man "Sorry sir

must be the wrong person he doesn't have any other children out there other than the

ones we have together." Shantelle sits back and thinks, this can't be real, and not him

he would never! Not on me. Shantelle picked up her phone and called Dawn and

Cynthia to fill them in on what had happened once Jordan had left for the day. "Girl you

are lying? Not the Jordan Dunkin, man of the year he would have never." Cynthia says

too the two ladies on the phone. "I'm calling my job and letting them know what is going

on because I can't believe his ass right now. After all that we have been through he has

been out here slinging his dick around the fucking city and now some petty bitch want

what I have worked all these years and hard months for , Oh Hell NO!!!" Shantelle rants on before hanging up the phone to call out for the day. Calling her job Shantelle says "Sorry I won't be in today I need to take care of a family emergency." Now Jordan is not answering but she knows he is working and he would never cheat. Shantelle decided to stay home yet she moved her car so Jordan doesn't know that she is home or that she didn't go to work. Its 3:45 the time he usually comes in with the kids and I hear the keys.

I'm in the basement waiting he is coming through the door I hear the kids with him ok so nothing has changed someone must have used his name those papers were wrong. Shantelle stops mid thought, WHO'S THIS CHICK?! Wait I hear another voice my kids can't even count past ten so I know that he done have no bitch in my house. No he wouldn't cheat must be his sister cause she comes over from time to time. This can't be real! He would never fuck another woman that wasn't me. Stepping up on the third step who could this be in the kitchen cooking for my family cause she don't look like his sister, mother or me the only three women who should be in this house!!! She looks great OMG!! her body maybe he is trying to surprise me and she is a chef cooking a meal for his family; cause he wouldn't cheat! WAIT PAUSE!!!!! (Is this bitch stupid all avenues point to the fact that this nigga is doing him while she is out working her ass off and YES WILL HE STEP OUT?) OK so here Jordan comes in the kitchen slides up behind the chef (his side bitch) and starts kissing her on her neck. Wwhere are my kids?!! Whyat the fuck he kissing her. Busting through the basement door "Who the fuck is this Jordan and what the fuck is going on?" "This is my friend.", Jordan replied. Well what is she doing in my kitchen cooking for my kids?, and explain this court paper for a paternity test.", Shantell screamed. "WHAT THE FUCK!! I THOUGHT YOU WOULD NEVER DO THIS JORDAN!!!!", cried Shantelle.

Game of Lies:Hidden Truth

"Paternity test I never fucked another woman!!!! let alone I havee never ran up in nothing raw other then you Shantelle so for some bitch to try to take me for a paternity test." Jordan tried to explain." You must have thought I was boo boo the fool? Cause for so long we were doing so well nothing had changed up and nothing has been off until today when that man brought this paper here Jordan. I always thought that you were the one who was going to change my life for the better and give me the life that I always wanted. I gave you parts of my life that no one else had Jordan. I trusted my life with you as my husband and you are no better than the life I ran from years ago"., Shantelle cried to Jordan. Trying to hold her and console her Jordan tries to hug herim but Shantelle pushes him away. "Go be with thatis bitch you got in my house cooking and fucking you while I am off at work, you're are a trifling ass bastard.", Shantelle argued. Pushing her way to the bedroom Shantelle storms past Jordan. "Shantelle please help me understand why we can't just work this out? Pplease! I know I fucked up but we are so much stronger than this. Baby I will leave and give you space but as my wife please baby don't leave me!, Jordan begs (pleaded). "Jordan listen to me and understand this, you were my dream you led me to believe that our family was everything to you and that you would keep us from all hurt, harm and dange;r but NOOOO you wasn't happy with just one woman I guess your no different from your bum ass father JORDAN DUNKIN JR!", Shantelle said as the tears fell from her eyes. Now knowing that her perfect life wasn't so perfect Shantelle decided to get her things and go stay in her friends guest house for until she could afford her own place.

Chapter 4

She can't leave me!!

As he sits on the side of his bed watching her pack though pack her things up into totes and get her things packed up to move out. Thinking it's finally over. Jordan can't stand this feeling that he has as he watches his wife pack to leave him and not for another man. He decided to cheat and be sloppy with what he was doing while she was away at work every day. Bringing that chick into his home and sexing her in the bed that he shares with his wife. Having her cook those meals for their children and lying to her like he was the one in there cooking that dinner she was eating every night. Not to mention also having her and keeping that house so clean for them. He was a great husband to her. Shantelle never thought that her man would cheat on her not even for a moment. She always believed him even when she thought that's not true you aren't cooking that where did you order that from? But she believed her man at all cost. *WAIT*, another child outside the marriage and another random chick in her house that he could possibly be fucking OH HELL NO!!!! Can Jordan explain what is really going on? From a court notice for a paternity test to another bitch in the kitchen cooking for their kids? Wait, Wait do you remember that Shantelle was hiding in the basement and watched it all unfold as she saw her husband her man come in the house with their kids and another bitch that she don't know? She walked in on them kissing in her kitchen. What happened when he turned around and saw the look on her face?

It was priceless to see how everyone was looking at each other. "So who is that woman at the stove cooking that good food? That is the good food that she eats every day not even knowing it." "So who is She DAMIT?" At a loss for words neither of them could seem to speak. No one could have pried the shit out of either of them.... not him not even her. Shantelle starts asking question after question "Who are you miss why are you cooking in my kitchen and where are the clothes that you walked into my house with? "WHO THE FUCK ARE YOU????????!" "Still dead silence nothing but dead air and she is getting hotter and hotter with the two of them. As they just stand there in Awe that she is even standing in the kitchen with them and caught them red handed. "Well since no one will seem to answer me I will just assume that you're the side chick that I thought my husband will never have and you have been fucking him while I'm at work at night because nothing else makes since to me, you're clearly not a maid dressed in a thong ...

"HOLD THE FUCK UP!!!!! a thong and bra cooking where the fuck are my kids while this thot is in here dressed like that?", Shantelle screamed at Jordan. Bitch if you don't go get dressed and get the fuck out of my house I'm going to fuck both of you'll up." Shantelle said with rage in her eyes, Jordan stands and says "Baby wait her clothes are washing she is not my side chick and I wasn't kissing her I was smelling the food I was going to try to surprise you tonight with a threesome remember my home-girl I was telling ran with me this is her." "What the fuck Jordan, you made this bitch sound ugly as fuck and umm she is far from ugly!!! Get your shit and leave I always told myself you would never cheat. And I stay home and look you got some THOT ASS BITCH in my house cooking in my fucking kitchen and you telling me that you haven't been fucking her in this house picture me believing you. I don't!!!" Shantelle storms out the room. Coming back in the room she starts again "then on top of that you have a fucking paternity test that was delivered here today for you and you going to lie and say that someone else used your name too I guess.. Hell no Jordan, I can't take this shit no more. What is really going on out there in them "streets" you out here sniffing pussy while I'm at work busting my ass fuck out of here? You got me downstairs in my own house stalking you and this bitch just to see what you are doing while I'm at work.", she confessed. "Wait babe where is your car?", Jordan questioned.. "FUCK that car you telling me that you worried about a fucking car when I just caught you in the house with a random bitch.", Shantelle said(countered) "She is not random she is my friend I told you that we run together and she wanted a threesome and we had talked about it so I thought I would be cool to try to surprise you tonight with it that's all." Jordan tried over and over to explain himself again. Shantelle wasn't e is not buying it that she responded, "We didn't talk about shit you asked and I never said yes. " Jordan is stressed sitting on his bed thinking I'm over the bull shit thinking that she would never leave him. He watches her as she storms out the kitchen and tointo the basement and then to into the storage room and grabs every tote she can grab. I'm done with this bull shit I'm OUT!!!!!!!

Shantelle goes to the room and she starts to take the things out of the closets and the dresserser draws, trying not to slam anything because she didn't want to wake the kids from their naps. He sits there looking like this can't be real we have been through so much and we have been married for over 15 years and yet I'm losing her. Jordan trying to stop her so many times "Baby, can we talk about this." Jordan says in this soft voice. "There is nothing to talk about you decided to bring some random ass chick into our home for God knows how long and have her cook for our family let alone you allowed our children to see you with this Hoe and you say it's a miss understanding

GET THE FUCK OUTA HERE!!!!" Shantelle says. As she is packing she hears footsteps thinking that the children are awake she gets quiet, however through the door comes the girl. OMG Shantelle thought that this bitch had left and to only find out that she is still here now this chick is trying to explain herself there is nothing that she can say that will make my wife stay I think that I have messed up and that now my marriage is so over he is so afraid that anything that she says will hurt his marriage even more.

The girl (Anastasia) walks in the bedroom saying "I'm sorry for intruding but I didn't know that you were unaware of me coming over here every day, in the beginning, I started out coming here getting paid for beingas a basic maid. getting paid I was working for your family cooking every day and cleaning for your husband." Hold up her what? Basic where Bitch? " I'm heated keep going you did what? Cleaning and cooking ok and keep going and then what. (standing in the middle of the floor pissed, I want to know WTF this bitch got to say and it better make sense) the girl continues "Then one day we were sitting at the table talking about that and about me making more money so that's how I got in the streets with him to do runs for him and do some accounting things for his men that are out there. I was never here to break up your home or to bring a wedge as I only came to only look for work." (So how did she find this family, I'm confused where did this THOT come from? So now my wife is like" Shantelle jumps in and ask, "Just tell me this how many times have you been fucking my husband?" in fear of answeringshe answers her question she answers.

Anastasia finishes telling what was happening "Last week was the first time that I had slept with him it wasn't on purpose I mean the kids were sleeping and I had come in to clean your bathroom and he was in here watching porn and jerking off I tried to ignore

Game of Lies:Hidden Truth

him as I cleaned your bathroom; I even closed the door to the bathroom so I could clean in peace. Next thing I know he was standing in the door way of the bathroom with a hard dick asking me why did I interrupt his man time? I didn't know what to say so I said nothing and turned around and started to clean the tub out. He began to stroke his dick in the doorway and I still tried to ignore him as my pussy was becoming wet and throbbing what was I to do?" Jordan started looking at his wife as she told her the story and the look on her face was like. Wait a minute was this a porn or was she telling the truth? Shantelle was standing there thinking, let me know because this story she is telling is getting hotter by the minute. She looked at her and said "I'm confused so if you ignored him then how on earth did you end up sleeping with my husband I want to know? And was this the same day? I need answers right now!!!!" Anastasia said "No ma'am it wasn't that day I left out of your room and left the house immediately."

Shantelle looked at him and said "So you in here trying to fuck another woman that you hired to do house chores and cook that you did not discuss with me from the jump, WTF?" Jordan couldn't find the words to reply. He couldn't figure out whether or not he should agree with her story or make her look like she was a big ass liar. Jordan cries to his wife, "Baby listen that was a big mistake on my part it was last Wednesday when you and I were beefing and I didn't have sex with you that day so I was horny and I tried to get some from watching porn then she came in here and my judgment went out the window. I'm sorry that I went that far with her but she was looking so damn good when she was bent over cleaning that bathroom and I already was hot from watching that porn, But like she told you baby I didn't sleep with her." Shantelle looked at him and yelled "THAT DAY!!!!!" So as they all stand in the room the silence comes upon the room no one is speaking.

Dawn and Cynthia show up at the house to help Shantelle with her move and the babies. Jordan pulled Cynthia to the side and said after all these years you still stick by Shanny side like you are really her friend. She just doesn't know how much of a friend you are not does she? She would flip a switch if she only knew what you did when she was away in college." Cynthia and Dawn carried everything to the car for Shantelle and Dawn put the babies in her car so that it would be room for all their things in Shantelle's car. Cynthia walked over to the two ladies and asked, "So when did he really cross the line and fuck Anastasia?" Without a straight answer Shantelle looks at the girls and say "Let me leave because the way things are going I feel like something major was ripped from me and that really hurts. I cannot believe that Jordan would allow pussy to come between us and our marriage, after all that we have been through."

Chapter 5

IT'S A NEW DAY!

Two weeks have past and Shantelle have moved out from Jordan and took the kids and a moving van after figuring that she would never get the answers she was looking for. Flashing rage in her eyes, leaving her house as she moved the last box onto the truck. Shantelle tells Dawn "I can't believe that over some piece of ass my marriage ended with one quick boom! He would have never told me that she was working here or even that he had slept with her and still I don't know the tail end of that. When did she sleep with him and how did this nigga think that he was going to get away with it? I have so many unansweredun-answered questions and after all that I have been through Dawn this shit hurts really bad. I want to just die right now."

Crying and upset not knowing which way to turn. Stressed to the max Shantelle figured she must just take her time and write in her journal because she can't talk to the kids they will never understand what I am feeling. My whole life has changed in the blink of an eye. Did I make the right decision should I have believed him and stayed? WAIT where is the answer to that paternity test court paper that came in the mail I never got to the bottom of that! But I refuse to call him and ask him anything right now he is on block and I have nothing to say to him. This nigga been fucking some random chick in my house that he "hired" and then he got to have some random ass kid outside of our marriage that I never go to the bottom of so I don't know what he thought was going to happen I was always taught what's done in the dark must come to light. Now I'm sitting here with these babies thinking that I have lost it all. If I express my feelings to him he will think that what he did was all good, but and he really fucked up our family that son of a bitch isn't shit. I never thought he would cheat. Guess I'll get to writing all these years and now look at me.........I should've must expressed myself through paper and not through loving my man.

April 8, 2016

Dear Diary,

She stole what was never yours

Why is it that you get mad when you see the chick with your ex?

Because in your heart she stole what was never yours from the beginning because if he was you would still have him. A fill-in is what you were in your heart. Little does she know that you completed him for so many years that even when your not paying him any attention he is in your bushes with no camo on? After all the years I invested into him he decided to cheat on me with this tramp who at one point was his side chick or the house maid so they claim. I feel like I deserve so much better but where do I get it from and who told her to come into the picture and take what's mine. Without any just cause claiming that they were planning something special for me and what was that a damn threesome that I never agreed to so where do I stand now all alone. She didn't steal anything from you that was yours that's what my inner self keeps telling me but did she come in with the agenda to take something from this whole situation? But my inner self says you're hurting because he was never yours from the jump. Just because this is the first time you saw him with another doesn't mean this is the first time that he said fuck you, wake up honey years yes I understand but you're not stupid he

Game of Lies:Hidden Truth

used you to get where he needed to be. Those kids? As they always say mama's babies' daddy's maybe!. Stand tall dust yourself off and take this time to regroup. Get to know who you are again and regain what was lost from this nothing in life is ever that bad that you can't stand up and get back on track. Your strength is within yourself. Let no one take your focus and you will succeed. And always remember some lost in life are actual gains. Pay attention during the lession and you will pass the test. This is not a lonely period this is a period of healing. He was conniving and he was cheating, but used money to cover his flaws all you could see was his dollars. Routine is key!

Signed,

I lost my life

Now she feels like all isn't lost but when she sits back and starts thinking about how she got to where she is, she cried just looking at her purpose. She always said I wanted to give my children a better life then what I had but this really isn't fair how could he break me like this?

The phone rings (Unknown caller).... "Hello" a female voice is on the other end, "Yes how May I help you."" This is the Baltimore County Western district police department." What the police what could be wrong she thought why are they calling me? What could this be about?

I do not understand why they are calling me what could they really want with me. Yes, this is Mrs. Dunkin, How may I help you?" the officer on the other end says "Ma'am this is detective Washburt from the Baltimore County Detention Center. We apprehended a young man today by the name of Jordan Dunkin who states that you are his next of kin." Shantelle looks at the phone and thinks what has Jordan done? Why has the law caught up with him? Maybe it's the drug game they caught him in a wrecked spot? I'm so confused. Shantelle mind was going so fast that she didn't even hear the officer say that she needed to come down the station and pick up all of Jordan's belongings cause they are keeping him until his bail hearing. All she heard was he should be calling within the hour to speak with you." Shantelle hung up and called Dawn and Cynthia telling them about the phone call and that she had just spoken with a detective about Jordan and that something really big had just happened. She was so nervous she didn't know what Jordan had done. Shantelle slams down the phone after speaking with the girls she was all over the place.

Game of Lies:Hidden Truth

Chapter 6

Watch out for the Boom!

Oh God Jordan is now in jail I don't know what to do, guess I'll call Anastasia and see if she knows anything. As the phone goes straight to voicemail serval times she become more and more confused about what is going on. I guess I'll stop pass to see if she is home before I get the kids and drop them at my sisters. Driving down the block so much is going through her mind what is going on why is my life spinning out of control why is she not answering me? Pulling up to the house its yellow tape and people with cameras, and an older lady is coming out of her front door crying. Shantelle and she is so confused about what is going on. She parks her car and begins to walk towards the crime scene when she is stopped by the detective, "May I help her ma'am?" "What has happened here sir? This is my friend's house what happened is she ok? ", asked Shantelle. "No ma'am your friend is dead she was murdered earlier today." "NOOOO, this can't be true murdered! Huh by who? What Wait murdered. I'm confused Murdered. Her Sshe is dead? Murdered?", Shantelle inquired. ? "No this can't be what has come of my life she is murdered and Jordan is in jail. Is she the reason he is in jail? NO HE WOULD NEVER KILL! Jordan didn't kill Anastasia she must have got into something that she wasn't supposed to be in. WAIT where is her car? Oh God I knew I shouldn't have started going out and hanging with her what if they come after me next because I started running with her? Oh Lord.", she sobbed. "Hello Dawn, girl you are not going to believe what the fuck I just found out or should I say put together. Jordan must have been the one to Kill Anastasia because I pulled up to her house and there is yellow tape everywhere and the officer stated that she had been murdered last night but that is all that they told me. Girl I am so confused right now I got to go get my babies and drop them off at my mothers and then go to work. Lord this shit is too much for one person to deal with Dawn! Aam I going crazy or Is this really my life right now?" Shantelle began to cry while talking to Dawn. " Calm down sweets it's going to be just fine you didn't kill her and she was only in your life because of him the relationship that you and her grew to have was out of loneliness honey I know that Cynthia and I have been so busy so we understand but don't beat yourself up over no bitch that didn't even appreciate your marriage from the jump." Dawn rebuttedrebottled.   Going straight to work from there Shantelle forgot to pick up the kids and she forgot to drop them at her sisters her mind was blown she couldn't even see let alone think straight.

   BOOM!!!!!!

Hitting the car in front of her she never stopped at the stop sign in front of her she is all over the place. Blood everywhere coming to in the ER at University of MD medical center, why am I here?.... what has happened to me? She pushes the call button for the nurse. "Mma'am what's happened and wwhy am I here?",Shantelle asked. "Ma'am you blacked out and hit an eighteen wheeler on Milford Mill Rd after you ran the stop sign.", replied the nurse.. "Ran the stop sign where was I coming from? Where was I going?", Shantelle pleaded. "Ma'am can you tell me your name?",the nurse requested.

 "Shantelle Dunkin I am 36 years old I live at 8448 Rockbridge Road Pikesville; MD 21208 my number is 443-552-9999.", she responded. "Thank you for that. May I have your next of Kin please ma'am?, the nurse investigated. . "Jordan Dunkin, My husband. His number is 443-888-7796.", Shantelle said. "Ok thank you", replied the nurse., Hhours pass and no one comes to the hospital not Jordan nort her mother and she can't

Game of Lies:Hidden Truth

seem to locate her cell phone. OH GOD my kids where are my kids? Her sister is

probably worried sick about her and she is in the hospital. and Fustrated then she

turns on the hospital TV. After talking to her sister and finding out that no one ever

picked the kids up from day care she was worried sick. Her mother has picked up the

kids and her sister was on the way. A face shows up on the channel 13 evening news.

It's Jordan her husband, the caption reads. "Arrested for murder of a young

Randallstown woman Jordan Dunkin, is charged with first degree murder of Miss

Anastasia Hareborn, age 26. The reporter stated that she was found dead in her

Randallstown apartment with nothing on but a robe over her bloody body.

Shantelle screams as she sees that her husband has been charged in the

murder that she thought was all a nightmare and caused her to black out. Her sister

rushes in the hospital room and breaks down as she sees how bad her sister looks she

is so upset she heard about Jordan on the radio on her way in to the hospital. "I can't

believe this shit so Jordan has murdered some young lady for what Shantelle.",

demanded her sister. "Crystal il'm not sSure what has happened because we broke up

about a month ago, long story short but I started to get close to the young lady that he

murdered as a matter of fact really close we were hanging out almost every night after

about a month after I left. Hell we stayed in the strip club at least one night a week. One

night we got really drunk and we went back to her place and I allowed her to give me

head, and before you ask.... nnot I'm not gay just got caught up that night but was

scared that she was going to look at me different but she never did.", confessed

Shantelle. ""WAIT WHAT", Crystal replied. "Yyou did what? Llet some bitch do what to

you?", she added. "Yes Crystal I did. Oh SHIT!!!!!" Shantelle yells out "I totally forgot as I was driving to see Anastasia the officer that had called me stated that Jordan was going to call me in an hour before I had blacked out at that stop sign. FUCK!!!!" Shantelle was so lost. "So much has happened I'm so not sure if he has tried to call me but I swear I'm so lost right now if Jordan goes to jail for a long time what will I do in life without his support and now that she is gone to no one will be able to get the kids or anything like that. WAIT my kids where are my kids Cry's?" "Dawn has picked the kids up from daycare and they are on their way to her house until you get out of here. She told me that she changed her schedule around at the office so that she can keep them until you are done in the hospital and you are able to function again." Crystal stated. "Crystal I swear that I feel like my whole life has changed right before my eyes causing me to think that I am living in straight hell, my life has gone from heaven to hell." Shantelle explains as the tears fall from her eyes. "What could she have done for Jordan to have killed her? She wasn't that bad of a person I swear she was a true sweetheart. Poor girl was trying to get her life together and he goes and plays God and ends her life and now his own daughters will have to grow up without a father." Shantelle looks out the window to the hospital room thinking about everything that she has been through and now the silly fight that she and Jordan had the tears fall even more.

Lord, please deliver me from my own sins because I have fallen oh Lord, In Jesus name Amen as Shantelle sits in the hospital bed and prays. The next day when the sun comes up the murder was all over the news from channel13 to channel 45 Fox was talking so much about the murder I had to change the channel. Dawn text Shantelle telling her to turn on the news and they should tell what happened the night that the girl was killed and what Jordan was charged with.

Game of Lies:Hidden Truth

The Article is out Early on Wednesday August 13, 2015 Baltimore County Police was called to an apartment complex in Randallstown MD. Officers found Jordan Dunkin,36, of Pikesville, MD in the home of Anastasia Hareborn,26, Mr. Dunkin called 911 and the tape from the 911 operator stated that Mr. Dunkin called in and said that it was an accident. She is not breathing its blood coming out of her mouth my girlfriend is dead I can't believe that this has happened. I love her I didn't mean to kill her I swear I didn't mean to kill anyone. What have I done. Shantelle was reading the paper thinking what the fuck I have been played from both ends Jordan was still seeing her and calling her his girlfriend and shit. I can't believe that he had me thinking that he had left her alone trying to get me to come back home. Crazy I thought that she truly cared about me being there for me when no one else was there and now it all comes out once he has killed her. Guess my grandmother was right all good things do have to come to an end.

Chapter 7

Your Days Are Numbered Son!

Months have passed since Anastasia death. It's three days before Jordan goes to trial for the on this murder. He calls every day to speak to the kids. Since moving back into the house things have been strange. The routine has changed up for the kids and I, nothing has been right since August. Since Moving back in the house things have been so strange coming home just the kids and I routine all changed up nothing had been right since August. Christmas is next month and thanksgiving is in two weeks first of many without my love. (phone rings) "Hello, good afternoon may I please speak with Mrs. Dunkin?" "This is she how may I help you?' " Mrs.Drunkien this is Theodore Blum from Bbloom and associates." " Yes sir how many I help you?." Shantelle answered with the confused look on her face. I'm calling you today to discuss your settlement that I have to offer from your accident, See Mrs. Dunkin the driver took fault so the company has agreed to pay you $67,000 but after all medical fees and lawyer fees you will clear approximately $47,580. Lord my children would be set if only Jordan was home. (Phone rings) "Hello" "you have a collect call from the Baltimore Ccounty Ddetention Ccenter. To accept this call press eight.", "the recording states. "Hello baby did you do what I told you in the letter I sent last week? Did you speak to Junior about that? Did Chuck bring the money for the lawyer that has to be paid tomorrow? Did Pun drop of the deposit for the week? By the way I don't trust that nigga so watch him, I think that Pun is a snake and that he will fuck my wife." Jordan goes on. "Well hello to you to Jordan, how are you good that's good. I will be up there to drop everything off tomorrow as matter of to the fact that I have to go to see your lawyer tomorrow and pay the balance on your bill and your loan. I went to Harbor bank and opened up a new account in just my name that way I can keep up with all the deposits. And what's this about you not trusting Pun if you don't trust him why do you have him coming around your family? Get your shit together and leave me be Jordan everything is going straight over here.", Shantelle stated.

"Bbecause right now he my only loyal that doesn'tdon't mean I trust his ass around you and my daughters; that's why he is to only drop off the money and pick up the envelopes from you and not come into the house or past the front door. Do you understand that Shantelle? Do you understand me?" , Jordan says in his demanding voice. After that call shantelle couldn't dare tell Jordan that Pun was going to be the one that was bringing her to the court hearings all week in order to reduce the cost of parking. The trial has gone on for over three weeks and today is the day that the sentencing comes down. Jordan Dunkin we sentence you to 26 years and that's with all but 18 dismissed leaving you to serve all years with a possibility for parole in 10 years with good behavior. All Shantelle heard was 26 years. Leaving the court house Pun asked "Shantelle would you like to go to the Windsor Inn for a few drinksing." Two crab cakes and fries, later after over 4 shots of patron and and way over 3 beers later, Shantelle was drunk as a fish. Driving to her house Shantelle caught Pun dosing off so and she suggested that he needed a nap. "Stay here until you sober up or at least until you get a brief nap?", she offered. Pun responded "I'll be just fine I think that I can make it home or at least around the corner." "Ok I'll stay for a few" pun replied. Walking in the house Shantelle was thinking what shouldwill I I do? I need a short nap so I'll go in my room and take mye clothes off and watch a little porn until I pass out.

Game of Lies:Hidden Truth

Hearing the sounds coming from Shantelles' room Pun was trying to rest until he and figured out what was she doing in there. With the sounds fromof the porn that Shantelle was watching. It was louder then she realized but she didn't really care she was horny and she was trying to chum because it had been so long. As theAs Shantelle moans from Shantelle becomes louderas she climaxed; Pun gets up to see what's going on in the other room. Shantelle had left the door cracked but enough that he could see everything that she was doing from caressing her breast to playing with her clit. Standing there watching Shantelle Pun realized that his dick was extremely hard and that she is way sexier without clothes on. Watching as she licks her fingers and get to working on the ability to making herself cum. Sshe thought that she was alone until she was about to cum and looked up and saw that Pun was in the doorway.r aAs creepy as it seemed s it that was also hot at the same time. Shantelle closes her eyes and starts to play with her pussy even harder until she sees that Pun isn't leaving that door way so she gives him a show from sucking on her own breast to fingering her pussy until she climaxes and calls out his name. "Ummm I'm Cumming Pun OOOH Pun." Shantelle screams. With fear in his eyes Pun runs out the door to the car thinking that he could have just fucked her and he got scared because he knows that Jordan would have his ass on a platter. Text message from Shantelle the phone reads "Why did you leave out the house like that? aAre you ok? I'm sorry If I made you uncomfortable it won't happen again It's just been so long since I have been fucked." "I'm sorry I couldn't get myself caught up in that Ma'am because I would be dead. " Pun replied. Thinking damn now I'm not going to be able to get her off my mind FUCK!!! He bangs his hand on the steering wheel. His phone goes off (text message) a video sent by Shantelle. Pun stops driving and started watching the video and starts to caress his dick and he wants to go back and fuck the shit out of Shantelle. Pun keeps going until he comes really hard in his car. Umm Shantelle hears the door thinking that her video made Pun come back." She asked form "Who is it?" It better not be Pun cause he is going to get fucked tonight. Who is at her door?

It was Dawn at the door with the kids, "How was the trial? I thought that I would hear from you once you got home from the court house." Dawn said. "Naw, I came in here and passed out I was so tired from sitting in that court room and listening to that judge and then to hear that they are going to give him 26 years and for what I might add? Because Jordan swears to me that he didn't kill that girl. Amazingly he didn't look worried at all about the time so who knows." Shantelle explained trying to debate whether or not she was going to tell Dawn what had happened when Pun was at the house. Sitting down and having dinner with Dawn and the kids they began to discuss the happy text that Cynthia had sent out about her pregnancy and that she was almost 5 months and didn't even know that she was pregnant. This Chick is crazy having a baby with that crazy ass boy she been fucking with Lord our little niece or nephew is going to be crazy just like her." Shantelle says as they laugh together.

Days go by and Shantelle notices that she hasn't gotten any money or calls/text from Pun. Knowing that's strange she thinks she should say something to Jordan when he calls. Funny a knock at the door maybe it's Pun coming to give her the money. "Who is it? She runs to the door with a big smile on her face and just in her robe. "It's me Shantelle? The voice on the other side of the door says. "Me who? That's not Pun's voice. "It's me Jason answer the door please" Jason replies on the other side. Now he knows damn well that I don't like him so why is he even here? Opening the door. "Yes Jason what brings you here to see me?" Shantelle says with anger in her voice. " I'm now the lead I am now responsible for the drops and the pick-ups. I'm also responsible for the payment of the monthly deposits and the new house guard when George needs a night off until further notice. Jason explains. "What the hell? What happen to Pun he was doing a great job and never disrespected me so what happened to him?" Shantelle asked. "About two weeks ago somebody got a picture of him leaving here with his pants open then they saw him sitting in his car jerking off to some video that came to his phone.

They reported it to Jordan and he decided to order his death since he disrespected him as his right hand man." Jason explained it all to Shantelle. Sitting in the kitchen in tears and she is going through it right now. "What do you mean he didn't do anything to me. Wwe didn't sleep together and who ever running their mouth should have come and seen me because nothing happened that day that he was in here watching over me after Jordan was sentenced.", she cried. Shantelle is all over the place in confusion from all that Jason just told her. "So I'm going to see Jordan and get to the bottom of it and figure out why he did this and didn't even speak to me about what was going on from here when he is in there. Ugh I hate Jordan ass right now." Shantelle said in full anger. "He took you off of everything off of his visiting list and his phone list he said that he is done with you he thought that you had cheated on him.", explained Jason. "I can't believe that his ass talking about somebody cheating on him when that nigga clearly cheats on me with these bitches in the streets. I just can't with him. I am done!!!!!" Shantelle says to Jason as she is sitting at the table crying and crying. "Wwho you talking about? Towanda?" Jason asked. "Towanda!, My cousin Towanda your ex

Girl?! He fucked with her? You'reyou are lying Jason! Pplease don't play with me that

bitch is crazy I know he didn't cheat on me with my own cousin!. OMG! Jason please

help me understand this." Shantelle asked. Jason sat down and started spilling all of the

beans to Shantelle from how he caught them fucking one day when he came in the

house and how she told him that the baby wasn't his but he had to claim him because

Jordan didn't want her to know that he had cheated with her cousin and got her

pregnant. Jason continued to explained to Shantelle everything that had happened with

Towanda and Jordan to the point where Shantelle stood up in the middle of the kitchen

and said "It's all good I will win this watch he will not win this shit right here out here

killing niggas cause he thinks that I'm cheating but this bitch can suck and fuck who he

wants I'm over Jordan Dre Dunkin Jr. FUCK HIM!!!!!", exclaimed Shantelle. Dawn

wakes up from all the screaming running to the kitchen to make sure that everything

was ok with Shantelle. e Sshe looked and saw Jason and being so surprised to see

Jason Dawn ran up and hugged him. They haven't seen each other in over 20 years

since she had moved away. "What's going on with the two of you that you have to make

all this noise and wake the sleeping people in the house?" Dawn asked. "Jason was

down here filing me in on some bull shit and now he was just about to leave but Im

going to go hop in the shower and you and him can catch up. Thank you Jason for the

information." Shantelle makes her way out of the kitchen and up to her bedroom.

     Sitting in the kitchen catching up with Jason Dawn sits at the table and makes

moves on Jason like she wanted to sleep with him. "So what you been up to Miss

Dawn? I see that you are all grown up now and not that little knock-kneed little 8 year old running behind me on your bike anymore." Jason says as he laughs. "Naw I'm all grown up now and I can show you better than I can tell you by the way." Dawn responds. Dawn was leaning over the table talking to Jason so that her thong shows from under her night shirt and trying to get him aroused. Jason leans over and looks not once but a few times telling Dawn "You are making my dick jump you better stop before I fuck you on this table right here or take your little ass in the other room and attack that pussy." Grabbing his hand and guiding him into the family room Dawn removes her nightshirt taking her shirt off while walking into the other room. Pushing Jason on the floor Dawn pulls down his pants as she climbs on top of him and slides and makes her way on to his hard penis going up and down. Covering his mouth with her hand as she strokes his dick with her pussy so that Shantelle won'tlle don't hear them. Little do they know not knowing that Shantelle was already on her way down to the family room and had stopped on the steps and was watching the show as her best friend had her way with Jason on the Family room floor. Shantelle watched from the dark steps as Jason turned Dawn over and planted his head between her legs and began to lick her until she was about to cream all in his mouth, then he worked his way back up and slowly put his big throbbing dick into her wet pussy. Shantelle worked her hands on her clit as watching them made her horny she couldn't believe what they were doing in her the house but they didn't stop. Seeing Shantelle standing there playing with herself turned them on even more the two came in unison with a loud breath of release.

CHAPTER 8

THE YEAR CAN'T END LIKE THIS!

Tomorrow is Christmas all done shopping for gifts nothing left to get, dinner is prepped and the is complete gifts all wrapped. Shantelle and Dawn are getting dressed for the strip club annual strip club Christmas Pageant that Jordan started years ago, this is the time when the club makes its their most money. Walking into the club with her best friend by her side dressed to kill, Shantelle notices that it's super packed from wall to wall. Dawn looked at Shantelle and said "Damn Shanny niggas be in this strip club like this, YOOO I never thought Jordan had shit popping like this I might need to work here during the holidays the way these bitches getting money tonight." The dancers were s are getting money left and right. Shantelle checks the back private rooms where each room goes for $750 for an hour on the pageant night. Every room was packed as well. The accountant told Shantelle that the club was already well over $2500 in revenue and they have only been opened for an hour and fifteen minutes. "They are going to be opened tonight for an extra hour so if they are making that money now", Shantelle says "Imagine what we will produce by 3 a.m." Shantelle was happy with the outcome of the club. Even the local radio station was there playing the mixes from 10-12 midnight. Every baller was in the club from Delaware, Baltimore, DC, and Virginia.

After a long night at the club Shantelle and Dawn stayed and closed the club and then makes their way back to Shantelle's place for the night. Shantelle was smiling from ear to ear the club had tripled its usual revenue for the Christmas Pageant. Many years in the past they have cleared $7,000 or better but this year the club ended the night with a revenue of $33,978. "Home Sweet home" Shantelle says as she pulls into her driveway. Dawn notices that is a box outside the garage door she got out the car thinking that it could have sent it could be something to hurt Shantelle and the kids, so she reads the box to see where it they could have come from. Shantelle was really scared to open the boxes and It was one box from Nordstrom's, one from Tiffany's and one big box from Christian Louboutin. When she opened the box from Nordstrom's it was two Burberry outfits with and matching shoes for the twins and with a card in there that read "Merry Christmas babies from Daddy, I love you see you Lil ill ladybugs soon. Then in the Christian's box was three pair of pumps with a card that read "Merry Christmas to my Lotus" Shantelle read that card about fifteen times. Lotus was the name that Anastasia called her; so if she is dead who the hell sent that gift to her. Then she opened the tiffany's box and inside was a bracelet with the twins names engraved and a matching necklace with her and Jordan's names and their wedding date on the back. The card read " To my better half of my life my shining star love, your husband". Shantelle was sitting there in shock and told Dawn "I can't believe that Jordan would send me a gift from jail when he has decided to turn his back on me. I guess I should remain grateful and show him real love and appreciation"

Christmas has come and gone everything was and all cleaned up and now they was getting ready for the New Year's Eve party at the strip club. Slipping on her tight black dress and stepping into her new Christian's she got for Christmas. Shantelle was in boss mode, although going alone wasn't in her plans but with Cynthia was home pregnant and Dawn was with her new boo; so that left Shantelle alone foron New Year's. She was ready for anything that night sexy wasn't the word for her as she stepped out of her car and into the club. Shantelle walked into the club and scanned the room club as she always does looking around the club to see who was in the club. Noticing that it when she stepped in that the club was just as packed as it was for the Christmas pageant. She went to the back to check the private rooms she recognized noticed that most of the girls were dancing in a circle in the VIP section, and on the books for the night no one had reserved the area so who could be that important to be in the VIP without a reservation. The dancers saw Shantelle coming towards them and they moved out the as if they were dancing for a king, and when they moved out the way Shantelle saw that it was Jordan her husband in the club that night.

Not even six months in the Baltimore County Detention Center and good ole Jordan Dunkin Jr. is out. Shantelle asked "So how long have you been home?" Jordan looked at her and said " Can we discuss my home coming later once we leave here right now its money to be made." " Oh ok so you coming home with me tonight? " Shantelle asked with a big ass smile on her face. Then she heard the horn go off for the New Year, 10,9,8,7,6,5,4,3,2,1... HAPPY NEW YEARS!!!! Shantelle reaches over and kisses Jordan as she wished him a happy new year. "I will stop by moms and get the girls if you want me to" Shantelle told Jordan. " No I will get them in the morning and surprise them." Jordan replied.

Riding home on high thinking about how I was so surprised to see Jordan in the club tonight and then to have him right here beside me as I drive home into my driveway. I haven't shared my bed with another man since I left Jordan back in July. He wasn't even gone a year and he is back home to me. We have been through so much but I'm pleased to still be called Mrs. Dunkin, Jordan Dunkin's wife. Walking into the house smiling from ear to ear Shantelle was ecstatic about Jordan being out of jail she couldn't think of nothing else. Washing the dishes from earlier that day Shantelle tells Jordan so sit in here and tell me what's really going on with you. I want to know everything from why you murdered Anastasia to why you wouldn't have called me about this thing with Pun staying here. and somebody sending you a picture of us together or something like that?" Jordan started spilling the beans on everything from the lock up to the murders. He told her that who all the murders was a set for a big drug bust trying to set Leo up for trying to take over the blocks and the neighborhoods. Anastasia wasn't really dead she was living in Mexico in a small town near Cozumel with Pun as her protector. He told her how he was an informant for the FEDS and that they had to fake everything and that the woman that was really murdered was a junkie that they had paid to die. With so much disbelief on her face Shantelle didn't know what to believe she was just sat sitting there at the table most of the night catching up. Then they noticed that the sun was coming up and that they had been talking all night long. "Let me go hit the shower", Shantelle said. "Put on something sexy for me baby I want to see you naked for sure. I ain't fucked in months my dick needs some attention". Jordan said as she walked into the bathroom to get in the shower with her. her shower. Getting out the shower and stepping into the room to please her man Shantelle notices that Jordan is knocked and is sleeping like a baby so she didn't want to bother him so she allowed him to rest. The phone rings Shantelle reaches over to grab it before it wakes Jordan. "Hello", she answered " Yea bitch! I heard that your bitch ass husband is home! Sso is he ready to have this test done so that I can take his fucking money. I don't want him! Bbut I damn sure can use some of those thousands." The female on the other end said without taking a breath. "Who is this?" Shantelle asked but the caller hung up on her.

Shantelle pissed rolled over and started to caress Jordan's penis talking it in her mouth and waking him in a fashion that she had never done before. "Umm yes ma, I love that warm mouth around my dick." Jordan moans. Before she knew you know it Jordan he was climaxing everywhere." "Girl you will not believe this shit Jordan Dunkin is home and he showed up to the club last night and girl once he gave me the run down oh my goodness, Dawn we must do lunch this week." Shantelle texted to Dawn knowing that she wasn't going to answer if she called her ,on the phone because she was out for the night with her boothang. Walking into the room Jordan asked Shantelle would she consider marrying him again because he really had fucked up this time.

Chapter 9

The dead has Arisen

I been hiding here in Mexico for over six months I'm tired of it for once. Every day I get up and I journal cause it keeps me at peace. My family thinks that I am dead the only one who knows is my cousin Jason that I am alive and well and that's because I am running with the same team as him. I have found that having this time alone has opened up the fact that Jordan and I made this plan and it all back fired on me while trying to help a man that will never be mine. I have tried to reach out to him and hope that he would just listen to how lonely it really is over here in Mexico. I sit up all night and write to keep from crying because its times that my journal is all that I have to keep me from going crazy. I love my babies that God has blessed me with but other than them I have nothing. I sit here daily and I write in my blog about love. Late night I sat up and wrote a love entry into my journal.

April 3,2016

The gift of lust

Who ever said that loving me would be just that easy?

Then I started to find myself looking for reasons to call him and to have him come over just to be in his space. Asking my round table crew am I crazy this man does not respect me nor do he notice me in public but in the bedroom he treats me like I am al that he has what am I doing wrong ladies please help...

Listen here.

When a man truly wants you it doesn't matter who sees him with you or who even knows that you are together. What's his deal is he digging in another bush somewhere or dealing with his past because something just isn't right.

Not too sure how to answer the questions without telling them that he is truly an ass and is still married to his ex along with the contact that they have is on an everyday basis or even that you just done trust him but something about him causes you to love him the way you do putting him even before yourself? The questions that you ask your self are going to be nothing like the questions the round table will present. What will they say?

So let me get this straight this guy loves you in private, plans the future with you in private and then has the nerve in public to act like he don't fuck with you? Well from some points he tried to explain that he leads a private life and what goes on in his house and relationship is his business, until you waiting and you hear things that you told him during pillow talk and around the city. Girl wake up and get yourself together no man nor woman is that important for you to love more then you love yourself and broken you will take on anything to call love and not focus on all of the signs that are in front of you. Understanding that you have to know what it is to love yourself first will make for a better you and a better relationship with anyone. To be honest you don't even love this man hell you don't even know him at all. Your lust for him has taken over your heart and your mind a man will come in and take over the venerable at heart. Stop giving people the power over your happiness and your love, delete him out your phone and never look back stop making excuses and let him be. You will be some much more at peace without a no good begging ass man in your life.

The round table feels that this guy is not a good look for that he is not at the level you need in life to bring you he is a constant let down and weight that you truly don't need.

Oh did I tell you that the round table doesn't cut cards the truth and that's all that they offer for you.

By. Anastasia Hareborn

I can't believe that Jordan left me here to raise these twins alone. He call himself being a good father by so called protecting me from the streets so he sends me down here with Pun's ass thinking that will help something what the fuck just me the twins and uncle Pun. I know that Shantelle has friends at home but she had become that best friend I always dreamt of and now I can't even talk to her fuck my life right now. I have been sneaking and sending Shantelle gifts but she don't know that it's from me because I'm not sure if he is signing the cards the way that I told him to sign them. Oh how I wish that I could contact her and tell her that it's me so that she would know that I sent them all from my heart. Shantelle kept me grounded for so long from being in them streets at night looking for money to coming up in the world once I met Jordan and started working for him, I have been blessed in more ways than one but now I'm back to being lonely. Phone rings "Yo! You woke it's time to get up you have an appointment at 11:30 I will be there to get you in about 10 minutes." Pun said on the other end of the phone "Omg Pun I need at least 30 minutes. "Anastasia replies 'Shorty I don't have 30 minutes to give you today." Pun said.

Sitting on the side of the bed thinking about how I'm hoping that the gifts don't scare her and she tells Jordan that she has been receiving the gifts. Wish I could just see her thought of sending her a flight ticket so that she could come see me and the twins I'll just act like the twins are by the guy I was dealing with before I was "Killed". She knows that we were trying to be friends and put all the negative behind us so that we could be genuine friends I had started to fall in love with Shantelle I miss her so damn much. Phone rings "Hello" Anastasia says. "Who is this?" the woman on the other end asked. "Anastasia is that you? Shantelle said. "Lotus, yes this is me." Shantelle said with pure excitement in her voice. Jordan told me that you were alive and that you were living in Mexico now and I told him that I needed to see you so he told me that I could make my way down to see you so I will be leaving Baltimore Friday afternoon about 1:45 p.m. and landing there around 3:30p.m. your time. I'm so excited we are going to have to catch up as soon as I get there. I heard that Pun was down there with you as well we are all going to have to catch up." After catching up on the phone with her lotus Anastasia looked at the clocked and noticed that it was 11:15 a.m. and her appointment was In 15 minutes. "OMG Lotus I have to go Pun is going to kill me I was supposed to be outside over 20 minutes ago. Anastasia said her good byes to her and hung up. Day dreaming the whole ride to the doctor's office Anastasia didn't hear anything that Pun was telling her about the phone call that he had just had with Jordan. She didn't hear anything about him not wanting them to hang together or nothing all she was worried about was seeing Shantelle in three days. Anastasia was on a natural high form her phone call.

Three days have passed and it is now Friday so excited about the fact that Lotus is coming today Anastasia was up early cleaned house and then took a nap around 1:30 pm. Resting so well when she woke and noticed that she no missed calls and that it was after 4:45 p.m. wondering where they were knowing that Pun was to be picking up Shantelle from the airport she was getting worried. Text from Shantelle comes open the door. Running to the door with pure excitement Anastasia opens the door belly first to hug Shantelle. Sitting around in her house for a few the three of them decided to hit the town and go out for dinner and drinks. Hitting longue and bar after bar they were drink as a skunk well Pun and Shantelle were. Offering her house to them for the night since they were so drunk and unable to drive anywhere Shantelle yells out' hey crew whatever happens in Mexico stays in Mexico." They all laughed together. Walking in Anastasia house they were laughing and joking. Sitting around talking until they all were getting tired. Going to bed Anastasia decided to shower Pun was going to sleep on the couch and Shantelle was going to sleep in the room with Ana. Thinking of that day he heard her watching porn and he watched her cumm to him watching Pun was so horny just being in the presence of Shantelle as was she when he came around her. Thinking she was going to play with him she decided to open the door to the bed room where he can see her undress and she started to give Pun a show and she started to drop her little black dress to the floor as he watched her still in her pumps she bent over and took her thongs off slowly. Stepping out of them one leg at a time keeping her pumps on. Taking her finger and entering her wet pussy she stands in the door way and plays with her pussy as pun watches on. Coming out of the shower Ana saw Shantelle giving Pun a show so she did want to disturb she climbed on the bed and started playing with herself once Shantelle noticed that she was in the bed she climbed on the bed inviting Pun into the room and she bent over and continued to play with herself turning Pun on even more. Turning her body around and inching her way between Shantelle's legs Ana began to lick Shantelle's Clit making her climax and right before she could cum Ana invited Pun to enter Shantelle from behind while she licked on Shantelle's' clit. Her body began to shack as she was about to cum hard as shit. "I'm cumming oh Shit Pun I'm coming." Shantelle whispered. Climaxing with her Pun releases as well. Dropping on the bed they all looked at each other and laughed. "It was a dream I had that I wanted to live out." Shantelle told them. Shantelle looked over at Anastasia and said "I hope that you enjoyed it mama. "By that time Anastasia was knocked out and she was sitting up talking to Pun half the night trying to figure out where their plan was going to come into play. Knowing that going into this as a team will help them get the empire that they are destining for. Day in and day out together these three became so much closer to the point where at dinner on Wednesday night before Shantelle booked the private jet, they devised a plan to take over Jordan's empire on step at a time. Not holding back nothing and leaving him with just that NOTHING!!!!! After all the shit that Shantelle had been through growing up and then for all the added heartache Shantelle wanted Jordan to feel what she had been through. Because, she felt like if he seen what having nothing felt like then he would beg for her to be the only woman in his life. To plan and to leave

him with nothing will have Jordan right where she wanted him to be.

Chapter 10

I am my brother's keeper.

Leaving the airport, I realized so much could go wrong with Shantelle going down to Mexico. At this point none of my plotting is working for the benefit of me. Giving me chance after chance to continue to hurt her Shantelle won't seem to go anywhere. Now I sent her to Mexico for two weeks hoping that she gets caught up somehow and wants to leave me. I know deep down I'm not the right nigga for Shantelle she deserves so much better than me. From me fucking other women to hiding kids by women to just sleeping all around Baltimore. Phone rings, "Hello" Jordan answers. "Yo Jord! All runs made, bout to go grab me this chick and hit it really quick then I got to meeting at 4:30 then I'll be in the spot." Danny said to Jordan. "WAIT the spot, you not taking the chick to the spot are you yo? Jordan asked his little brother. "Hell NAW! Reign is in the spot, by the way she just asked me to call you and see what time you were dropping the girls off to her so that she can have everything together as far as their dinner and stuff. I can't wait to see my nieces it's been a minute" Danny was so excited about the girls staying with him. Driving to get the girls from Shantelle sister Crystal and then feed them something Jordan decided to make a stop past and see if his home girl Syd was home he needed to pick up some stuff and she was on the way to Crystal's house "them Owings mills chicks swear they all that" Jordan said when he pulled up in Syd's driveway as she was getting out of her BMW with her new wedding band on. "Yo, you always talking shit and stuff but still lonely as I don't know what." Syd replied. "Lonely who not me I gets pussy left and right, bitches die to be with JD all the time but watch me whip watch me nae nae on that ass girl while your husband isn't home how about that. "Jordan replied. "Get out of here, where my girl Shantelle at cause I'm sure she doesn't know your ass over her trying to fuck your babymova." Syd said. "You are my best friend not my baby mother no one will ever know that Brian is not Amber father and that I am so hush and go inside and bend over for daddy. "Jordan replied. Fucking Syd quickly then leaving to go get the girls Jordan almost forgot to collect the gifts and money for the girls from "Auntie Syd". Thinking as he was driving down Rolling road there isn't one chick that I didn't have within ten feet of my zip code. Lord save me thanks God for condoms. Pulling up to Crystals place she brings the kids out to him both girls are sleeping. Damn its quarter after five I have to be to the airport by 6:30.

Rushing to get down to Danny house to drop off the girls Jordan gets an email stating that his meeting set for Saturday morning at the Barkdale reality company has been rescheduled to Monday and if he needs to cancel please respond to Mrs. Barkdale by Noon Saturday. Coming from Danny house it will take him 25 minutes to get to BWI. I can't believe that I am rushing like this because I wanted some ass from that damn Syd. She is my true first love but I can't believe she went and got married on me I'm hurt. Arriving at the airport rushing through TSA and to the terminal Jordan gets on his flight to LA. Just a few more hours and I'll be in the warm sun of LA. Texting Shantelle "I have landed here in LA safely I love you my heartbeat and I will check in on you when I get to the room my phone is dying so don't respond." Lying through the text Jordan blocks her number during his trip to the hotel hoping to get into a new chick tonight.

Walking into the Ritz Carlton LA Jordan is making his way to the guest services and he bumps into none other than the beautiful "Taylor Barkdale". Dressed to kill body like a god she fine as hell. "If it isn't the Jordan Dunkin Baltimore's most wanted FBI informant biggest drug king Baltimore has seen since the early 80s." Taylor looks at him in awe. "Damn Taylor you looking edible I mean good. "Jordan laughs. "Thinking I wasn't going to see you until Monday morning, I got the message that our meeting had to be rescheduled due to you having an emergency." Jordan said. Not an emergency but I do have to be in Vegas tomorrow un some unexpected business for two days. "Taylor responds. "Would you like to get a drink Jordan asked. "I have to go up to my suite and settle in if you want can grab a bottle of wine from the bar real quick and you can come up while I get settled in." Jordan offers "Sure we can catch up I was on my way home but no rush I'm home alone tonight so no problems." Taylor replied. On the elevator up to the 20ᵗʰ floor They catch up a little bit on the elevator about the events since his father Jordan Sr. got killed and she moved from Baltimore in 2002.Life haven't been the same since his father died in his apartment in Woodlawn. Taylor asked "Your married now right?" " I'm not married anymore my wife left me two months ago and ran off with my homeboy and some sleazy chick that I once ran with, I don't know if you remember my homeboy Jason from chocolate city his little cousin Ana? That's who my wife left for Mexico with and then told me that she wasn't coming back left me with the kids and everything letting me believe that she was going for a weekend and didn't come back. Can we not talk about this cause it's still fresh so it still really hurts. Jordan explained with real tears in his eyes. Taylor felt so bad for him she reached over and hugged him. Walking into the room Jordan puts down his things and opens the bottle of wine. They continued to catch up and Taylor says to Jordan I'm still crushed by how bad Danny hurt me when their son passed away in the car crash. Telling him that she wanted him to love her and he wouldn't. Jordan reached over and started kissing Taylor whispering in her ear "I'm grown now and I'm not Danny. I am my brother's keeper but I and not my brother I won't hurt you just let me show you and make real love to you right here right now baby."

Jordan started to rub his hands up Taylors back. She whispers "Umm Jord please I can't do this, I'm not ready to fall for you like I did your brother, umm your touching all the right spots your making me hot Jord. Softly licking his fingers then fingering her love box as he works his way down to her belt button stopping and working his way back up. "Um Damn" Taylor moans. Taking his tongue and licking slowly around her clit making her squirm. Jordan waits until right before she is about to climax and he slides right on into her making her cumm all over him. "Taylor can I make you mine?" Jordan ask. Collapsing on to the bed together they lay in each other's arm as good as it feels it's beyond wrong. Taylor woke up to leave out at 6 a.m.. Try to make her way to her car leaving Jordan in the room asleep. Taylor makes her way to Vegas. Walking in the MGM she greets her husband Jordan Dunkin Sr. with open arms.

Chapter 11

Empire Will Expire

Being in Mexico for this past few weeks has given me the chance to clear my mind. I have been able to get so much started in operation take over Jordan's empire. He has plotted so long to hurt me with kids all over Baltimore some hiding in VA and now twins by Ana. I know he don't think I'm just that dumb. When he told me that he had business meeting in LA. I called my little sister and told her to intercept his true mission. Jordan forgot I'm from the same ole hood he from that chocolate city crew was never nothing to fuck with. He taught me everything I needed to know hanging with him after school and riding from west to east and helping him rob niggas and take over the city like his father used to. Sometimes I think that he thinks that because I got this good education that I do not have the common since to get over on him. I filled Dawn and Cynthia in on my plan and that I might need them to help out. Cynthia is not really been herself lately but that's possibly due to her pregnancy, but my bitch Dawn offered to follow Jordan to LA to keep an eye on him she is the shit to me Dawn will ride or die for me I swear I love my real chicks. With this $120,000 cushion I already have and diverting 64% of the club's earnings into my new account. Jordan won't see this shit coming. Waking up with a fresh frame of mind this morning that text from Taylor made my day. "Got em" Jordan has no idea that he sleeping with Taylor just costed him half of everything that he owns right now. That mission was fool proof (phone rings) unknown caller Shantelle presses decline. Phone rings again its Jordan. "Hey babe how LA?" Shantelle asked. "Weather is great food good too just everything is high as shit out here everything cost so damn much money." Jordan replied. 'So tell me what's new in

Cozumel? Did you meet new people and did you find anything exciting on the beach?" "No baby It's been a great break for me to clear my mind." Shantelle replied. "Babe you come home on Tuesday right? I wanted to know because my trip was extended until Monday night because my meeting has been rescheduled for Monday morning. The owner had an emergency so they had to reschedule my meeting. "Jordan told Shantelle. Reading the text from Taylor, "that nigga can eat the shit out of an ass though sis I am not lying to you though." Laughing out loud Shantelle tells Jordan "Imma call you back cause I need to hop in the shower and get ready before the sun goes down I'm going to a beach party." "Good night my love" Jordan replies. Shantelle hangs up the phone without saying bye to Jordan or even saying anything in response. Laughing to her self Shantelle started thinking, what will happen when he finds out that Taylor is married to his father who he thought was dead over 7 years ago. This shit is getting crazy but funny is you just can't beat a girl at her own game. I slowed down my life for Jordan and loved him for everything he was to me but little does he know that before him the games that he thinks he Is playing on me I have played before. Looking in the mirror thinking I'm a boss and best believe that when you see me you see me stepping as a boss. Sliding up her lace black thong and her black lace bra. Stepping into her yellow Christian Louboutin's and her all black body con dress hugging every right angle and every right curve Shantelle walks out of her new condo like that boss she had become. Driving to her dinner for her business meeting at the Restaurant in town Shantelle realizes that if this goes through she is will become more then a millionaire she will be everything she always wanted to be and not have to share any of it with Jordan. Trying to open three new businesses in Mexico at the cost of American dollars will be awesome for her. Shantelle walks into the restaurant turning heads left and right. The young lady she is due to meet stands up getting her with a kiss on the cheek. "Well Hello Ms. Dunkin you look stunning" Michelle stated. "The pleasure is all mines Ms. Young. I would like to thank you for taking your time on this busy evening to discuss this matter. I am so excited about buying these properties and getting the show in the road." Shantelle stated. After discussing all the matters of business Shantelle walked away with one of the biggest smiles on her face when she found out that she would be making an access of over 2.6 million dollars. Texting Pun and Ana when she left "I must say today was a good day."

There is nothing like, driving down the road blasting the radio listening to Lauren Hill taking it back in the day for a minute. Just thinking about where she has come from and where she is going. Looking down at her phone she saw that she has a text message from Pun. Shantelle reads the text and a great big smile on her face. "sitting here thinking about you I can't seem to get that video you sent me months ago off my mind and I can't even stop thinking about how you felt when I entered into your wet pussy. Damn baby you got me going I'm just hoping that this doesn't fuck up how you look at me but I want to taste you one more time." "I'm driving back to my condo now I have to stop past the market and pick up a few things I was going to cook me something to eat let me know when you are on you're on your way." Shantelle sent to Pun. Making her way back into the Condo Shantelle hops into the shower and lays across her bed awaiting Puns call and she passes out. Waking up an hour and a half later Shantelle looks at her phone she realizes that she has missed 10 called and two text messages form Pun and Jordan also called while she was sleeping. Texting Pun

"I'm sorry babe I passed out on you I took a hot shower and passed out putting on

lotion. Hopefully it's not too late for you to come over and chill with me.

Cooking a small dinner while waiting for Pun to respond to the text message

about coming over Shantelle started to think about how the things in her life has

changed so much from having a loving and caring husband to now trying to plot to take

his whole empire. Wait until Jordan finds out that his father is still alive and has been

running his whole cartel from Baltimore to LA without being traced setting up nigga after

nigga. Caught in mid thought Shantelle hears the knock at the door. Walking to the door

she opens it without asking "who it was" knowing in her heart that it was Pun. He began

to walk in the condo with a smile from ear to ear full of happiness and joy that he was

getting time with Shantelle. Pun is starting to fall for Shantelle but he knows that nothing

will come out of this beside great sex because she is only fucking him since she is in

Mexico but when she returns to Baltimore life will possibly go back to where it once was.

Kissing her on the neck "hey sexy how was your day?" Pun asked. "I had a good day

and after you fuck the shit out of me I will have a great night as well." Laughing

Shantelle says. As she walked into the bedroom Shantelle starts taking off her robe

leaving on nothing but her heels knowing that turns Pun on she bends over in front of

him and starts fingering herself. "Why do you tease me so Ms. Shanni?" Pun said in a

sexy voice. "Ummm I want you to come over here and take total control of my hands

and my body knowing that you can have me anyway you please Pun. I want you to lick

me and fuck me from behind and give me all of you deep inside." Shantelle whispered.

"Shhhh let me taste that sweet wet pussy Mami." Pun breathed as he entered his

tongue into her without a pause licking and sucking her until she cums all in his mouth.

Slowly working him into her and grinding until they climax together collapsing onto the bed and drifting off to sleep. Waking up about two hours later to Puns head between her legs Shantelle begins to moan she feels herself about to climax and explode when out of nowhere is a knock at the door. Who could it be at the door?

Chapter 12

Leo the lion

Business , business always business for Jordan Dunkin Sr. at the age of 62 still has it going on. Leo is running a multi-million dollar reality company and one of the largest Cartels that run from the west coast to the east coast. Jordan Dunkin Sr. Better known in the streets of LA as Leo Barkdale. Leo has ran both coast for the past 7 years since his so called death. Leo gets so upset when things don't go the way he has planned he is a very precise man and everything must go the way he has planned from business to the bedroom. Leo will fuck a young girls mind body and soul with just one line. He knows how to make them smile and at the same time he can make them cry.

Waking up in the MGM grand opening the curtains to the penthouse suite that is always reserved for the him and no other guest. Leo started looking back at the sun shining on his wife's body as she lies in the bed. Having a 37 year old wife that is totally in love with him makes Leo feel like a king or at least like the king that he is. The twist to this is that Leo's wife is Taylor the sister to his daughter in law and the mother of his son's deceased child. The plot will thicken before it thins. Leo looks over and saw that Taylor was waking up he reaches over and kisses Taylor greeting her with a "good morning beautiful." Taylor rolls over with a great big smile on her face looking at Leo in his face and greeting him with a big kiss and a "I love you my king." "My ladybug what are you doing today? I was thinking to send you and Jasmine to the spa today and then have the driver take you girls to get lunch and a pedicure. Maybe a little shopping or something simple you know how much Jazzie loves shopping. "Leo said to Taylor.

Game of Lies:Hidden Truth

"Matter of fact Jazzie just text me and asked which of us was going to come and pick her up from Monique's house they were about to shower and then have breakfast before I leave for the day." Taylor said. Watching Taylor walk into the shower turned Leo on. Going out on the balcony to have his morning smoke Leo answers a call. Hello I can't talk but I can text. Leo replies as he hangs up the phone. Reading the text that came through from Alex. " I'll be in Vegas tonight my flight is at 8:10 pm just making sure that you will be picking me up from the airport and that you will be also joining mw for dinner tonight as I haven't seem you in almost three months. Leo replies to the text message and says "Yes you will see me tonight I will be at the MGM so just meet me there near the entrance to the Rainforest Café. Gotta go Leo sends the message and then goes back into the room and into the bathroom to join Taylor in the shower. Whispering in her ear "Nothing like fucking your sexy ass in the shower." Lowering herself to the point where her mouth meets his manhood Taylor begins to give Leo some head making him moan really loud the shower action gives Leo a thrill.

Stepping out the shower Taylor asked Leo, "What time would you be flying back home on tomorrow because you know that Junior and I have a meeting Monday morning. I pushed it back because I came to see you for the weekend and I know you not ready for him to see that you are still living yet are you?" "I could care less if he knows that I am living but at the same time we have so much to do to get him to learn his lesson on using and abusing the Dunkin name so we will make sure that the game plan goes off fool proof." Leo responded as he sat there stroking his manhood watching Taylor dry off from out of the shower. Leaving the room to go start her day with Taylor kisses her husband and says her good byes until he returns home.

Game of Lies:Hidden Truth

Laying across the bed Leo dozed off thinking about how much his life is a mirror in his eyes through his son. From having children out in the world that were not just friends but close friends and not even knowing that they are really siblings. It's 8p.m. and Leo is late for his pick up from the airport Leo was supposed to go to the airport and pick up Alex one of his leading lady's for over 35 years. Leo and Alex were friends in high school then they decided to go ahead and make it sexual yet they never married or made anything official. Racing to get dressed and ready for Alex's arrival Leo finds the nicest things in his wardrobe and remembers that he forgot her yellow rose. He never greets Alex without a yellow rose. He knows that she would be so hurt if he didn't have her rose. Leo calls down to the front desk and he orders her a single yellow rose for when she checks in.

Heading down to the rainforest café to meet Alex for dinner and drinks Leo reserves a table at the private dining room in the MGM. Showing her a good time as always Leo spoils Alex with gift after gift trips and everything. Talking about her trip she just returned from asking about how she enjoyed all the surprises that he had planned for her and her friends while they were away in Paris. "Have you thought about the move I asked you to take to the west coast there is nothing left for you to do in Baltimore." Leo asked Alex. "Knowing that I am still hurting so bad from the death of Anastasia, My days are not the same Jason has finally moved out on his own and now living better but I wish it was a way I could get him from being up under his brother and his ring because Jordan will be leading Jason to a path of destruction. Jason asked me the other day how was his mother when she was younger and how is it that she lost her life giving birth to him. He wanted to know why is Junnie not there for him as a father but knowing the truth at times I want to tell him that I am living and so are you." Alex told Leo. "He must never know that I am his father let alone that I am still living. In your contacts how do you have me saved because no one must know that I am alive until that day when my guys out here take over that battle in chocolate? I heard yesterday that Brian was shot in the face while sitting in the drive through at the McDonald's on Coldspring Lane. What the Fuck is going on in the city baby that they are taking out all of my sons I must do something before my oldest boy gets taken off the face of Baltimore streets.

This drug game isn't nothing like it was in the 80's. Justin will be in from Hawaii on Monday morning to see you. I told him that you were in Paris and that Jordan was out of control from fucking bitches and using the girls to make sure that he sets his ass straight for me." Leo told Alex." Our baby is coming home after 22 years of being away oh God I haven't seen my baby in 22 years I can't wait to see him. I won't say nothing to a soul about nothing you can trust me daddy. "Justin asked me the last time that we spoke, Why were we so close and what was the investment in his life, I told him that his father and I were really close and that he asked me if anything ever happened to him would I look after him. I told Justin that I promised and I meant what I said promised Junnie that he would always be at the top of my list. I couldn't tell him the truth that I am his father." Leo stated. "The day I found out that I was pregnant with Justin I was so happy not telling you that we were having him and now that he is 40 years old all those years in the military kept my baby alive. Kept him out of the streets and out of trouble because the rate that the rest of your boys are going they are going to be dead. Jordan has a great business mind on his shoulders but he coming back out into the drug game was not the best thing he should have done. He has so much to lose if he ever gets

caught. But my oldest baby is coming home!!! " Alex said with excitement.

Making their way to the penthouse suite still catching up and talking about their

six children that they have together. Leo walks over to Alex and whispers in her ear "

let's just forget about all this real life bullshit and let fuck like we are high school kids

again." Pushing in the room door and kissing and touching before they could even make

it to the bed Alex pulled Leo's manhood out and straight into her mouth it went blowing

him so well that as he felt himself coming he throw her over the chair and rammed his

penis into her throbbing pussy making her cum so hard neither of them could move for a

good 6 seconds. Leo told Alex, 'that was the best sex ever baby but I have a

confession." Alex replied 'Yes daddy what is it." "Your daughter is alive she is living in

Mexico and she will be having twin boys come May. She has been there since last

summer and she is fine I speak with her often and Shantelle is there with her now." Alex

screamed "ALIVE".

Chapter 13

WHO'S ON TOP

Phone rings. "Hello" Jordan answers "Your car is ready Mr. Dunkin" the front desk said. Getting ready for his meeting before his flight, Jordan packs up the car, double checks that he has everything he needs for his meeting and his flight, and then checks out. Stepping out of the hotel and into his rental Jordan calls Taylor to confirm that she is at the office. After three tries and no answer Jordan begins to get worried, so he calls the office. "Thank you for calling Barkdale and Associates Reality Company, this is Cynthia speaking how "may I help you." "Yes, this is Jordan Dunkin and I have a 9:15 meeting with Ms. Barkdale is she available at the moment?" Jordan asked. "No Mr. Dunkin she is on a call right now may I put you into her voicemail?" "No ma'am I will be there shortly."

Walking into the building full of excitement Jordan gets on the elevator thinking he will finally make a name for himself just like his father did. "Good Morning Mr. Dunkin right this way Ms. Barkdale is waiting for you in the conference room for you." Cynthia told Jordan. "Good Morning Ms. Taylor how was your trip?" Jordan asked "Great had a wonderful time in Vegas, a spa day yesterday, and a great drive home last night." Taylor responded. Meeting with the realtor board and parking locations for possible club sites and a possible new casino. Jordan was on a high out of the meeting, he scheduled his next trip to LA for a month out, not knowing that Dawn already was aware of all the plans that he made and was in on the plans of Shantelle and Taylor. Going to the car Jordan calls Shantelle

with great enlightenment that they would be opening in LA and possibly in Vegas

with in the year. "Hello you've reached Shanni sorry I can't take your call leave a

voicemail at the tone." Voicemail picks up three times. No answer from Shantelle.

Pulling up into the airport and returning the car Jordan thinks about all that has

happened in the last year and where he has come from. Phone rings "Hello my love"

Shantelle says. "I called you three times I'm at the airport now heading back east to

Baltimore. Everything went well, we have to come back out here in June for the final

touches and since we are married I can't buy without you. Baby we are getting ready to

be on the map." Jordan told Shantelle with pure excitement in his voice. "That's a true

blessing baby; we will celebrate once you get back in town. I've picked up the girls and

we will be here waiting for you. I love you have a safe flight." Shantelle told him as she

hangs up the phone.

     Heading to the terminal Jordan realizes he left his phone in the rental; rushing

back to get it he almost misses the elite boarding for American Airlines. Going through

the airport Jordan notices a tall gentleman getting off a plane at gate A4 that resembles

his father looking really hard the gentlemen quickly moved through the airport. Before

Jordan could get close the man disappeared. Texting Anastasia "How are my little guys.

Wishing I could be there for you right now I would die to be the father to my father

wasn't to me. God knows that I would be wonderful father to my son's. Let me know

when you ready to order all that is needed for my boys I want to spoil them to death.

Guess I'll text you later when my flight lands in Baltimore, Love J-Dog. Listening to

music on his flight Jordan realize he was just like his dad with all his plots and schemes loving this woman and that woman. But Jordan could never forgive his father for the death of his mother. Jordan remembers it like yesterday when his father chocked the life out of his mother because he found out that she had slept with Junnie and got pregnant with Daniel. Till this day Daniel has never got a chance to meet Junnie - his biological father-. So much is going through Jordan's mind on how he always wanted to be better than his dad and ended up just like his dad. Thinking if he could get one chance to just speak to his parents again.

The flight attendant comes around with chips and drinks "would you like a drink sir?" She asks "Yes can I get a vodka straight" Jordan says. "I need ID and credit card please." The attendant asks. Bringing back the drink she says. "Here you are Mr. Dunkin, funny is I had an older gentleman with the same name on my last flight to Vegas." Jordan looked with shock on his face. "You sure miss?" Now he all over the place was that man his father; Naw my dad is dead. Laying back in the chair Jordan begins to dream of when he was smaller and he was with his father in the streets and when they would come home to his mother and baby Brother Daniel. Jordan saw his father image and heard his father's voice calling him. Waking up and feeling the tears fall from his face and just remembering the good times that he had growing up as the son of one of the city's biggest drug lords. Life wasn't always perfect but all the girls love the Jordan Dunkin he was a track star in high school and always had the latest things but, never claimed any of those chicks but was always seen with that Shantelle Bacon girl. The girl who he made his wife after over 20 years of friendship and he almost lost after one night of sex.

Chapter 14

Once Upon a baby

My last morning in Mexico and so much has happened. I can't believe that I will be a mother in a few months and all I have to offer my babies is love and support my mother never really gave me. Knowing that Jordan really don't want my babies hurts me so much I will lose if it wasn't for Shantelle coming down and helping me get some of the things that I needed and having them shipped to my temporary place in Baltimore what will happen if Jordan realizes I am coming back in town for him. I have been writing in my journal everyday just so that the stress doesn't hurt my precious babies. I am so tired of hiding secrets. Tired of hurting and searching for love. My mind is all over the place if I allow Jordan Dunkin to stress me and my babies out we will be no better I need to stay away from him until I am sure the coast is clear. Dear God please protect my boys as I carry them and go through this yet another major move in my pregnancy. Guess I'll write before I hop in the shower and get ready to start my journey back to Baltimore.

April 17, 2016

Getting dressed thinking I'm not that pretty today look at my body it's just not that sexy. This pregnancy has me in my feelings about my body and my sexiness. My best friend is simply gorgeous she is flawless every man wants her. From strangers to people we have known for years she always turns heads and we are both the same size. Then a man comes and wants to talk to me and I'm asking myself 'What does he see in me? why do he think that all this fat is sexy?' my stomach hangs over my jeans I have rolls after rolls. I can't even remember when I was a size 8. look at me I just can't seem to feel sexy. Pretty face and would love to be think in the waist but the sexy kind these rolls are sexy! LOOK AT ME!!! I'm just not that pretty.

Applying my makeup maybe that will help me feel pretty, putting my perfume on maybe that will help me feel pretty. Knowing that my face isn't ugly but my body got damn it's a mess. I have two sets of breast a size 12 in women's not a junior size anymore and I am not that sexy two kids later he still says I'm beautiful even when I feel I'm not! Maybe I'll start saving my money and I'll make life easier if I'm not skinny but sexy. Gym running excising everyday one hour a day I can do this I got this I'm going to make this happen. I'm going to be that size 8 again watch me I'm not going to eat past 7 at night no more sugar no more carbs I got this I will be skinny by the spring I will not fail. Sexy I will be I will be able to wear that two piece once I hit that beach. My friends will look at me and see that I am determined to change how I look cause right now I'm just not that sexy. I tried and tried I can do this, from nutritionist to nutritionist from doctor to doctor diet pill after diet pill I will change how the world sees me. They will see that I am not just a chunky girl who wants to be skinny but that I am that sexy woman walking with confidence.

OOPS

  Nothing seems to be changing I am now only a size 10 and it don't seem to fell sexy even thought I know that I am carrying twins something just don't feel right. I can't seem to get this out of my mind my self-esteem is so low right now. I can't seem to get that sexy I was searching for. What am I doing wrong I have exercised every night and every morning I eat right I take my vitamins and I stopped all sugars and sweets. It's been six months and the scale is saying I lost 25 lbs. but my body still looks that same. Everyone tells me that they see that change in my size but I can't seem to find where they see it at. I just don't feel sexy anymore. Maybe its cause I can't find the right fit in clothes, how is it that me and her both wear a 10 and hers looks fabulous on her and I look a mess. Maybe it's all pregnancy talk or maybe it's just that I'm just not her!

Anastasia Hareborn

Jordan has broken me so far down to the point where nothing in my life seems to go right anymore. Getting in the shower with a face full of tears Anastasia can't seem to think straight today. Not knowing which way to turn she is full of doubt and pains for the future of her twins.

Phone ringing she rushes out of the shower to answer. "Hello" she says as she is trying to figure out who could be calling her. "Good morning my love did you get my text the other day about the boys and what they need? I was flying home and thought of you I miss your feelings and how it wonderful it would be to see you give birth to my boys. Ana I'm so sorry that I have put you through so much. I always wanted to be a better guy then my father was when I was growing up. I know you are not used to me pouring out my heart but I swear I think I truly love and miss you." Jordan says. "Jordan you wouldn't know love if it smacked you in your face twice. I only care about the fact that you make sure that my sons are well taken care of nothing more nothing less. Nothing else matters to me. I only want that life that you promised me I would have when I got down here. And Jordan nothing has been as you promised since you shipped my pregnant ass her. Listen to me and understand I knew that I would be a single mother and I also knew that no one would give me the life that you could being the mother of your children. Jordan you are a lying son of a bitch you told me that I would never have to lift a finger ever again and since I have been here both Pun and I had to go out and find work to take care of myself and my babies. The fucking Doctor you assigned for me was talking about putting my babies up for adoption because the living here is not suited for babies." Anastasia explained her pain as the tears ran down her face. "Let me explain Ana. I been running in and out of town trying to make a new so that my children will have the life that's they always wanted." Cutting Jordan off in his tracks Anastasia Yells. "YOU'RE FUCKING CHILDREN YOU HAVE SO MANY OF THEM THAT YOU CAN'T EVEN COUNT. YOU ARE NO FUCKING BETTER THEN YOUR FATHER HE HAD SO MANY KIDS IN BALTIMORE CITY THAT WE FUCK AROUND AND BE BROTHER AND SISTER." "What the fuck you talking about I am my father's only child since my sister past. I never listened to all that bullshit people would be talking about my father having all them children. The only one that was out in the world life that was my tramp ass mother she had Daniel by my fathers' fucking cousin with her trifling ass." Jordan said as you could hear the frog in his throat. "Dismiss me with the bullshit Jordan, you are a piece of shit and that's that. You will never be the king of Baltimore hell your sloppy ass going to fuck around and get caught. Running around fucking all them bitches in the city and thinking that Shanni will never find out about them. With you it's like 10 degrees of separation between your bitches." "Just let me know when you're done." Jordan says "I didn't call you for this Anastasia, Ill chalk it up as your emotions cause your pregnant. I never let anyone talk to me like that. You know damn well better then to sit around and think that you can just open your lips and speak what you please." Jordan said with Discuss in his voice. Slamming the phone down and yelling Fuck Jordan Dunkin. Anastasia begins to feel pain in her lower belly. Laying across the bed she sends a text to Pun " I can't take it I'm in pain I don't know what's wrong its way too early to have my babies. Come quickly use your key." Oh Lord please don't let me lose my babies as they still have 10 weeks before I should have them. What is this did my water Break? NOOOOOOOOOOOOOOO!!!!!!!!!!!

Chapter 15

Have it All!

I usually sit back and let Jordan take all the orders and run the game but since he has been away and left me in charge so much have changed. I have been waiting for him to approach me about telling Shantelle everything about him and Towanda but he knows better. I may be the get runner but I will lay his fagot ass down with no problem. This nigga keeps fucking all these chicks and thinking that its cool. Hell we can't even get a chick because of Jordan Dunkin having half the fucking city wrapped around his finger. Walking away from the McDonald's after he received the news that his god brother was shot Jason couldn't understand why they were really beefing with the Chocolate city boys because they had nothing to do with the arrest of their leader.

"Auntie, I have been going through so much since you have been in Paris. What time will your flight come in tomorrow? This way I will be at the airport in time to get you I have to pick Lj up from daycare for Towanda and then......" The voicemail cuts off so Jason couldn't leave his complete message. "Damn it she never answers her fucking phone what the fuck do she be doing? Ugh". Jason says in anger. This bull shit got my blood boiling right now. He feels his phone going off and its Shantelle texting him. "I need to see you." "what could Jordan's girl want with me I though the bitch don't even like me now she need to see me this better not be no fucking set up." Jason says to himself. Driving down Northern Parkway to get to Pikesville Jason remembers that Jordan is in LA so what could she want from him? I 'm going to go in here and check this short bitch cause she better not be calling me about no dumb shit I can't stand a stupid ass female. Sitting here following Jordan ass knowing that he ain't shit kills me.

Game of Lies:Hidden Truth

Pulling up in front Jordan and Shantelle house his head is not clear it's all over the place so he tries to get his thoughts together before walking into the house. Jason walks up to the door and knocks awaiting Shantelle to answer. She comes to the door with a big smile on her face. "Come on in Jason." Making sure that the coast is clear Shantelle shuts the door asking "You are alone right". Umm Yes Jason stated why wouldn't I be?" He asked. "So let me tell you about how I have found these Letters in the basement I don't think that Jordan has ever read anything that was in his mom's box because he really didn't want to see the truth but I came across this one and I truly needed to share this letter with you. Sit down Jason and read this please I think that this is something that you must know." Shantelle told Jason. As he began to read this letter Shantelle noticed tears forming in Jason eyes and his yellow skin turning red. The letter was written by Jordan's Mom to Jordan sr.

June 17,1981

Jordie,

To my loving husband I have tried for over the past 7 months to hold this in. I wanted you to know that I know everything about that baby you and Alexander has in November that little boy that goes to my sister's daycare center looking just like our son Jr. I believe his name is Jason. Alexander told my sister that Jason was her deceased sister's son until the months and dates didn't add up. Tricia passed away on Halloween that year and this baby was born November 17 of that year on his medical record he has no father listed and the original birth record has Alexander King as the mother. Jordie Now when I thought that the little girl was your Junnie told me I was wrong until one late night I followed you and saw you buying things for that baby out of K-mart on Wabash and I followed you to her house. I'm not sure what the truth is about him. So I took the liberty and got a sample of his hair and Jordan's hair and the truth is that he is your baby. I will be going to see Alexander tomorrow because that bitch eats dinner at my table and stays at my

house like she is my friend. You can't hide the truth forever Jordie.

Signed,

Your loving stupid ass wife.

Wait what! My aunt is really my mother? Are you sure that we are brothers or are you making this up Shantelle?" Jason looked so confused that he didn't know whether to cry or scream. " I need a drink and some weed." Jason said. "I didn't know how to tell you so that's why I called you over while Jordan is still out of town. Shantelle explained. "How so I look at my aunt the same I can't I don't know and now that means I lost my sister my best friend to my brother?" Jason is so confused with all this new information.

Phone rings. "Hello", Jason answers. "Jace this is Auntie Alex." Silence from Jason he did not know what to say to her. Jace" she repeats." Yea" Jason says with hesitation. "My flight comes in at 10 Am tomorrow I'll see you about 10:30 ok." Alex says to him. Jason hangs up the phone no good bye no nothing. What the fuck man this bitch been playing me for over 30 years like she my aunt and the bitch my mother fuck around I could have been fucking my sister or something. I'm all fucked up right now. Calling Dawn to see what she up to because the news just took him over the edge Jason pulls up to Dawns job to see her before picking up his aunt from the airport. "Baby what's wrong? You sound so upset when you were on the phone." Dawn asked. Telling Dawn about the letter and trying to hold back the tears Jason breaks down in her arms and tells Dawn that he wants to just run away from all this pain. "Baby this feels like I lost my mother all over again and this shit hurts so much more then you will ever know." Jason cries to Dawn. "Well baby I am leaving for LA in a few weeks I will be out there for a little over three months on business would you like to go out there with me and we just chill and start working on us? I don't want you to leave me but I also can't guarantee that you won't have to deal with this at some point in life baby." Dawn told him. "Ok Baby lets go I don't want life without you so I'm also willing to get away and decompress from all of this drama I know that in my life it has been so much going on but never thought that I would be dealing with this." Jason Said as he kissed Dawn bye. " I'll call you once I get off baby. "Dawn kisses Jason Good bye.

Pulling up to the airport Jason has so much that he has on his mind he don't know how to greet Alexander should he shock her and say hello mom or hey auntie? Waiting outside of the American airlines pick up Jason sees Alexander coming towards the car and he instantly breaks out in a cold sweat. Not looking himself she asks him "Is everything on Sweetheart?" "I'm not feeling myself right now. I can't explain what's wrong because I'm lost in who I am right now." Jason replies thinking he has said too much. Riding to the house in complete silence Alex says to him, "Your very quiet today is everything alright Jace?" "Just tell me one thing because I am beyond lost with some information that fell in my lap. "Is the late Jordan Sr. my father and are you my mother?" Jason looked in Alex face as he asked her. With a pale face and blank stare Alex don't respond. Jason grows furious "HIS HE MY FATHER ARE YOU MY MOTHER!!!!!"

Chapter 16

He would Never!!!

Shantelle is lying in the bed thinking that his routine has still never changed with Jordan. From the time that he showers to the way that he gets up in the morning and goes about his day. He thinks that he is so slick if he keeps his routine that was that it once was she will never think that nothing has changed. It has been a year since that day the Shantelle found out about Anastasia and so much has unfolded. Leaving out the house and kissing Shantelle on her forehead Jordan has no clue about the plans she now has for them. Jumping out of bed to watch him leave from the bed room window. Shantelle gets the kids up and dressed and leaves out knowing that today she is to pick up things from her P.O.Box she rushes to the post office. Picking up the mail and a few boxes she was waiting for. Looking through the mail and the videos from Taylor comes with pure excitement Shantelle calls her lawyer and makes an appointment for later today. Trying to make everything seem smooth Shantelle tries not the give any of her secrets away. "Good morning Mommy, I'm on my way are you ready?" Shantelle asked her mother. Driving down 70 to Fredrick to pick up her mother she was thinking about how she could just stop all this drama by letting Jordan know that she knows that his father is living. Not a bright Idea Shantelle let things play out as they may her conscious tells her.

Driving through the city spending the day with her mother Shantelle notices that she didn't hear anything from Pun or Ana about their arrival times. Shantelle text Pun, "Hey Pun checking in to see what's going on what time will you be coming into town?" Hours pass by Shantelle was so busy with running with her mother and didn't even notice that she didn't get a response. Looking down at her phone Shantelle decides to call Pun with no success she gets no answer and the voicemail is full. Wondering what's really going on Shantelle calls Anastasia and her voicemail pops on as well. Thinking that they just might be on their flights already Shantelle continues on with her day. Dropping her mother off back at home and heading back to Pikesville to pick up the girls Shantelle starts to just think back to that day in 96 when she met Jordan. He was a junior at Frederick Douglas high school. She was working at the Popeye's in Mondawmin Mall as a cashier. This fine young man came in there so much that Shantelle knew what he wanted to eat without him even ordering. Passing her his number one day and saying "call me shorty you're a true cutie". Tears started to form in Shantelle's eyes as she thought about all the trips and the dates how Jordan spoiled her from the first date but then thinking of where they were today hurt badly. The ringing of the phone distracted Shantelle's day dream she answered the phone. "Hey Cynthia girl, what's up?" Shantelle asked. Are you busy I need to talk girl talk with you can you come past or I can meet you at your house? Dawn and Jason are too busy moving into their place today." Cynthia said. Meet me at the house I'm picking the girls up in about 30 minutes then I'll be home just meet me there." Shantelle responds, hanging up the phone it never dawned on her that Cynthia was crying all upset and not herself. Pulling up at the day care Shantelle looks down at her phone it was a message from Pun. "Our flight had to be changed Anastasia has a pre term labor scare she thought that she was in labor. We will be leaving here Tuesday at 12 noon; If anything changes I will let you know." "Ok" Shantelle replies not realizing how short she was with him.

Shantelle goes in to get the girls and heads home. With so much on her mind Shantelle doesn't even notice that Jordan is home already and that Cynthia was parked on the street. Shantelle took the girls in the house and laid them on the couch both girls are sleeping. Hearing a noise coming from up in her bed room Shantelle thinks that she must have left the Television on cause she stay watching Porn. Until she gets up to the last step and sees Cynthia giving Jordan head. What he can't keep his penis to himself without fucking somebody she thinks. Waiting to see just how far it will go Shantelle pulls out her phone and begins to record as she watched Jordan and Cynthia have sex in her bed. From him giving her head to him flipping her over and hitting it from the back listening to her tell him that she was his and that her pussy was his Cynthia climaxed and started to Cumm Jordan screams out and you better not tell Shantelle that I fucked your ass in our bed. Hearing that Shantelle walks in and says too late you're busted! Saying out loud "My best friend Jordan I thought you would NEVER!!!!! Now I know that we hooked up and had a threesome once but to ever think that you'll were sneaking behind my back and had a sexual relationship is out of this world. I thought that of all people I could trust the friendship and bound that we had Cynthia being as though you know every secret in my life that no one knows and you know where Jordan and I are right now and all that we are going through and for you to do this is out of this world."

Chapter 17

Guess Who's back

Coming back from Mexico has me in mixed up right now so much on my mind arriving in Baltimore waiting for Shantelle to send the car for me at the airport I don't know how I will explain Anastasia absence. Should I tell her that she backed out should I tell her that she had the babies and couldn't come what is that Is should tell her or maybe just the truth. Nothing ever works out how we plan. I only have 3 days to give to these Baltimore streets before I must return to my sons. Jordan has always thought that those boys were his but I got news for him wait until I leave this on his door step. Pun had so much on his mind he could decide which way to turn. As he sees the car pulling up he sends Shantelle a text. I'm here will explain once you hit the hotel I'll see you at our meeting time." Shantelle responds to Pun. "You're alone? IS everything ok with Ana?" "We will talk when I see you." Riding in the back seat of the car Pun is reading his entire missed massages one from his mother stating that she was having issues with his little brother and that his oldest brother will be returning from Hawaii in a few days. She wanted him to give her a call she has been sick. "Wait what Jason found out that Mom was really his mom? Oh God I hope that she didn't tell him about the fact that Jordan Sr. was our father. The only one who really wasn't our family was Ana. The true story of Ana was that she was the lady down in Cherry Hill daughter that Mom worked for Miss Tricia. That was the lady died and she gave Ana to our mother. This is who we called Auntie my mom's "Sister". When she passed my mother told Jason she was his mother. Yet, Ana is Junnie and Tricia daughter but that has never been confirmed. Ana thought that I was Junnie son so she never really asked me about my parent that's why it was so easy to fuck her that night she was upset about Junior fucking Syd.

Walking into the hotel Pun sat back and thought maybe if I trick Shantelle into loving me the way that she loves Pun I can have half of everything that she is taking form Jordan. That bitch is so fucking sexy but she never looked my way when she was younger thinking that the big guy has no swag. Funny is now that I'm fucking her she looks at me differently. As he is getting in the shower Pun hears the door to the hotel room close knowing that Shantelle is due to come to see him he is rushing to get out of the shower. "Hold on Shanni I'm coming." Pun yells out. She walks into the bathroom and climbs in the shower behind him rubbing his manhood and making him aroused Shantelle begins to make all these moves on Pun to get him all excited. "Umm I missed your touch baby let's get out and let me taste you." Pun said turning off the shower Shantelle leads Pun to the bedroom part lying on the bed she allows him to start giving her head. Calling Jordan's phone on purpose Shantelle lets the phone pick up so that Jordan can hear how Pun is pleasing her. As Shantelle climax she yells out his name telling him to get on top of her and go deep. Pun listens and starts to grind in Shantelle's pussy not knowing that her phone is on she asked him "so tell me where is Ana?" "She is in the hospital in Mexico she had the babies yesterday evening and so that way she couldn't come, But baby can we talk about this after I cumm this pussy so good you got my dick super hard." Pun says. Not knowing that Shantelle has set him up she allows the call to go on long enough for Jordan to trace her call. Thinking this nigga just don't know I know that he is to real father of the twins and that Ana is dead from giving birth because the hospital called her this morning and told her that the babies are in foster care and that Ana has left her as next of kin and in her living will she will get the babies.

Not expecting anyone the door to the hotel opens and in walks Jordan. Knocking Pun across the head he stops and thinks Oh God I have killed him and I got to clean this up. Shantelle and Jordan plot to get rid of the body before anyone could tell what happens until Jordan phone rings the voice on the other end says, "Hello Son." In total shock Jordan drops his phone. I cannot even phantom the fact that someone would play on my phone like that picking up the phone Jordan says "Hello" the person hangs up. He couldn't seem to trace the call because the person called from a blocked number and that way Jordan couldn't call the number back. Running out of the hotel with so many un answered Questions Jordan was in total shock.

In the back of his mind Jordan thought that he was going crazy. "Who is it Jordan?" Shantelle asked him as she watched the tears start to fall down his face. " Hello, yes who is this?" Jordan asked the man on the other end of the phone. "It's your father I am alive son." Then the call dropped. Not able to trace the call Jordan was filled with questions. The man sounded just like his father but the number was blocked so he didn't know who could be playing on his phone. "I can't believe that someone would play like that, Calling my phone talking about "hey Son." Who in the fuck would play like that Shantelle?" Jordan asked as he then realized that Pun was still breathing. Knowing that they can't just leave the body there they both sit in the room trying to figure out what to do now that he is not dead. "Jordan he is moving" Shantelle says to Jordan. Wrapping his hands around the bed post so that he can't get up. Shantelle start asking Pun question after question. From how did he think that he could play her and Anastasia having them think that he was on their side. So afraid that Pun would rat her out Shantelle didn't want to ask him to much so she stopped asking questions so that he wouldn't rat on her plans to still take over Jordan's empire. Then stayed in that room until morning trying to come up with a plan to keep Pun quiet about the fight the night before. Jordan says to Pun "Please just understand that is anything else happens and your ass is in the middle of it you will be dead." "Ok little brother" Pun replies "Wait what I am not your brother, we are no longer anything so don't call me brother." Jordan replies as he walks towards the door to leave. "Don't believe that we are brothers, I'm sure your mother knew that Jordan Sr. was my father. Now ok little brother we shall see who wins." Pun replies. "Man Fuck you!" Jordan yelled.

Driving back home Jordan had so much on his mind that he couldn't figure out what was going on if he was going crazy or not. Thinking and what that nigga mean he my brother my mother knows that he is my father's son. My mother would have blasted my father before she died. Mind going and just thinking about his life how he went from having to go from pillow to post with his mother because his father was always on the go and forgetting to pay most of their bills. Jordan always promised himself that he would never be like his father only to be the mirror Image of him. Pulling up in the driveway Jordan mind was racing as he puts the key In the door to his house. Thinking so much about his parents. Jordan goes to the locked room in the basement where he kept everything that was his mothers. Looking at old picture the tears began to fall all the good days are coming back to him he is remembering all the good his mother did. Never letting them go without him nor Daniel. Opening up a sealed box that he never saw before Jordan sees a lot of writing on different sheets of paper. Jordan begins to read the writing on the papers. Shocked by the things that he saw that was really going

on with his mother helped Jordan better understand his life and why he was the way he

was now.

August 23,1988

Today is her birthday so I guess that's why he didn't come home tonight. Its 12:15 a.m.

and my son still has no milk but Jordie didn't know that I saw the phone calls and I watched him

go into Alexander's house with their two sons. That oldest boy looks more and more like my baby.

Oh Lord why am I staying with Jordie what holds does he have on me? Dear God please save me

from this life I have been loyal to Jordie and I have held him down when he was in jail for 15 years

on a drug charge. Taking Alex with me not even knowing that she was sleeping with my husband

and that the boys were his as well. I should have known though because Jordie will fuck anything.

Please save me lord.

Signed a broken wife.

Crying even harder finding out that Pun could possibly be his brother Jordan kept

reading letter after letter. The more he read the more he realized he was his father.

After coming across a picture in his mother's box that his father had taken.

Remembering back to 94 when he was in Disney World with him Justin, (James) Pun

Jason, and Daniel. Thinking back then that his father was extra nice allowing them to

bring friends with them only to find out 35 years later that these were his real brothers.

 Still going through the box Jordan finds a birth certificate that reads Dustin Dunkin born

May 10, 1996 died May 12,1996 born to Jordan Dunkin Sr. (age 42)and Shannon

Kimbrell (age 26). What who is this Shannon person? Wait. My mother passed away

that next day I came home from school and she was dead in her bed. May 11, 1996.

They told us that my mother died of natural causes but she must have been killed who

killed my mother or did she really die of that heart attack from depression. My father really killed her with a broken heart. What really happened to my mother? With so many unanswered questions Jordan calls Shantelle's Phone. "Baby hurry home, fuck that nigga I need you home right now." Before she could reply Jordan has hung up. Picking up the phone to call his Lawyer Jordan decides to hang up and try to find this Shannon woman himself. Walking upstairs to the bedroom Jordan eyes are red and he just can't put that box down his mother left him so many answers. His mother left so many stones unturned now what about his father his death left the world wide open but now Jordan is getting closer to finding out how his father died.

Chapter 18

Duplicate This

"My entire marriage Jordie has cheated on me, that late night in August when I thought that I was dying Jordie left me there to be with Alexander. I have been gone from the states and have been here hiding in India for years. I sit in this house and I watch my children grow up from social media and I have watched my grandchildren come into this world through pictures that Shantelle may send from time to time. Now it's time I break my silence I have raised my daughter here in India since I moved here she is finally old enough to find her real father. I know that Jordie is not dead I know things that he thinks he really got away with. I will be getting my thoughts together as I prepare to leave India for good and take my baby girl home to meet her brothers. China will walk through the streets of Baltimore with her green eyes and long black hair she will grace the city with the presence of a goddess. They will not even notice China as their sister she looks nothing like Jordie and she looks everything like a young me. I will be taking China to the airport tonight to catch her flight her room is prepared at the

Game of Lies:Hidden Truth

Sheraton near the BWI airport her rental car is ready. Watch out Baltimore a new China doll will be in town to take over the streets. "Asia says to her mentor group as she releases her hidden pain during her weekly group session. A sponsor in the group stands up and says "Asia will you leave and join princess China in the states again?" Not answering her question directly Asia just looks and replies "Only time will tell that the Queen will do, but best believe when I grace the streets of Baltimore with my presence they will all fall." Finishing her counseling group Asia starts her way back to her place to prepare to release China to the streets of the states. China has studied each family member knowing the daily ins and outs of the ones her mother has her to watch. "Shantelle will meet you at your room around 10 tonight she has something for you that will help you get close to your brothers. It's going to be a package that she has had of mine for years I know that she is looking into some permanent housing for you and I but we will not be directly in the city where they will see me until that day comes that we spoke of that night that we have planned with Shantelle."

Leaving India China has so many unanswered questions for her mother but don't know how she is going to ask them. She climbs on the plane and thinks that she will just sit back and enjoy this ride. Lying back getting ready for this ride her first layover will be in 6 hours as she sits in her seat and watches her movies until she falls asleep. Landing in Houston China has a 4 hour layover she decides to call her mother and let her know that her flight has landed in Houston and that she will call when she lands in Baltimore at 7:30 that night. China sits back and starts going through her Facebook page. She sees this guy who is friends with her oldest brother his name is Todd. Todd was about 6'4"about 240 lbs. and his status says single. Todd is dark chocolate and he is in the military last checking in at the airport in Houston China begins

to smile if I could run into this fine thing Oh my goodness I would die she says to

herself. The announcement comes on that her flight will be boarding all A-list fliers and

first Class China stands to get in line standing right behind this tall dark man with an

Army back pack and these strong arms she thinks what if that's him. Her heart begins to

race but wait he never said that he was going to Baltimore he only checked in here what

if he is landing. Boarding the plane China stays close trying to see the man's face. As

she sits down in her seat she is looking at her phone she is on Facebook looking at his

pictures. A deep voice says "Excuse me is someone sitting here?" not looking up

because she is so engulfed in her phone China says "no". Still looking in her phone she

continues to look on Facebook waiting for him to except her friend request she says

softly, "Oh what I would do to get to meet this fine young thing and he really is not that

old." "Oh really what would you do to get to meet me?" the deep voice says. China looks

up and its Todd. He was sitting right beside her with his good smelling cologne and his

handsome face. They began to talk and they talked the whole ride back to Baltimore

they got to know so much about each other before the plane was even at Baltimore.

Finding out that they were even staying in the same hotel Todd asked her to dinner she

declined for that night but she did offer another night for the dinner date and he

accepted.

Arriving in Baltimore they exchange good byes and part ways. Making her way

to her room after checking in China sees that her mother has called several times

knowing by now that she is sleeping China decides that she will call her tomorrow.

Nodding off in the chair after that long flight and talking with Todd China forgot all about

Shantelle coming to visit her. She was startled by the knock at her door thinking that it was Todd she jumped up and ran to the door thinking how did he know what room I was in. opening the door with a big smile on her face to see that it was only Shantelle, China's smile left immediately. Walking into the room Shantelle catches up with China giving her all the ends and outs of Chocolate city and the things that she will need to know so that she can get around the streets giving her the names of her sibling so that she will not run into them on a fly. China looked at Shantelle and said "why are you helping my mother take down my brothers if you are married to him?" Shantelle replied its not taking them down because Leo will be back to do that part but in order for us to take over the empire there are stages that we have to take to set things up the way that they are needed. My mother had this set in place before her and your mother left for India. I know that she is doing well. I have brothers in the game as well but we are tired of being abused by these men so we have devised a plan to crush their empire starting with Jordan because he is the one that everyone listens to." Understanding what she was speaking of China nods letting Shantelle know that she will do everything as it is directed between Asia and Shantelle.

Riding through the city making her way to the harbor China receives a text from Todd "I would sure like to see them green eyes today." With a great big smile she replies "And that Chocolate skin I tell you." Making plans to see each other later China makes her way back to her room to freshen up before Todd meets her for dinner. Pulling up to Arundel mills mall China phone rings she remembers that she had been in Baltimore for two days now and have not spoken to her mother. "Yes mother" she addresses the call. "My Princess China doll, you have not called me since you have made it to the States who has your nose wide open?" Asia asked. No one mother but I

am on a date with this guy I met in the airport. I will call you after my dinner. I love you

mother." China rushed her mother off the phone as she watched Todd walk across the

parking lot. Thinking how it would be to beak her virginity to him. Mind racing China sits

in her car thinking that she should invite Todd up to her room but the fear is that she will

fall in love like her mother did for the wrong person. After having dinner and catching up

with Todd over dinner they decide to go back to the hotel to finish there catching up.

Sitting in the room talking and watching television Todd puts his hand on China's

ass. Her heart skips a beat as she leans in and lays her head on his chest thinking will I

give him my body. When suddenly Todd's phone rings," Hold on baby I got to take this."

Todd said. Answering his phone "Yo, Jordan what's up man? I been in town for about

two days but can I call you back I'm a bit busy" he said. Sitting in the living room China

started thinking oh my goodness that is how I will get in good with my brother through

Todd. He will be my link to the streets that I will need to get answers to Jordan's

empire. Todd comes back into the Livingroom with China and starts kissing on her

talking in her ear asking her if she really wanted to go to the next step. Wanting him in

every way China turns her ass to Todd as in to say take it slow Daddy. Pulling her

thongs off and raising her dress above her head China pussy starts to jump she is

waiting on Todd to put his dick inside of her instead he takes his head and he plants it

between her legs making her cream all over herself and forcing his tongue inside of her

and she begins to cumm like never before not ever knowing what this is that she is

feeling she cumms time after

Sneak Peak

The Plot Thickens : Who Laughs Last

Chapter 1

On my way up!

Sitting on his flight back into Baltimore Justin is thinking about the last time he was on Baltimore. He has not been home in over 22 years and he couldn't tell you anything about the streets. Knowing that he is going to go through some hard times coming all the way back to where he ran away from 22 years ago. Justin looks over at his wife and says. "The hardest part about this all is I don't know where I'll start I still have hard feelings against my mother." Kimberly looked over at Justin and said "The only way to fix what's bothering you is to face it head on." "What if she don't approve of you or our children? Will she ever really tell me why I am going through some of these dreams I have had for years of her sleeping with Jordan Sr. all those years when I was young?" Looking out the window of the plane so much is going through Justin's mind. Not knowing if he should just chill for a day or go straight to see his mother. As the plane is landing Justin turns to Kimberly and says "Let's change our hotel from the Holiday inn near the casino and go to the Sheraton BWI that way If I want to get away from my family I can. I am just so afraid of how this visit will go baby." Kimberly agrees as the plane lands and they begin to disembark from the plane gathering everything and their twin girls. Justin is walking off the plane holding his 3 month old daughters in his arms one carrier in each hand. Kimberly looks back and says, "With us here with you everything will be just fine."

Heading into the city to see his mother Justin's phone rings, "Yo, big brother I heard you were in town for a few days." The young man on the other end says. "Yeah just landed on my way in town now to see my Mom, how are you and where are you right now?" Justin asked. Catching on that its Jason on the other end Justin yells out. "Jay is this you? Oh my God I really want to see you little cousin I can't believe how grown you sound I thought that you were Pun for a minute when you said big brother." Not knowing how to respond Jason says," You know I have always looked up to you as my big brother I have told you that from time to time." "Yo, meet me at my mother's house I'll be there in about 15 minutes. I can't wait to see you." Justin replied. " Naw that's not a good idea Yo I'm not really speaking to Auntie Alex right now so I'll pass but we will catch up in a few. Just hit me when you are about to leave her house and I will hook up with you." Jason explained. Hanging up the line Justin is wondering what has happened that Jason and his mother aren't speaking it must be deep because Jason used to look at his aunt just like he was his mother. Looking over at his beautiful wife as he pulls up to his mother's house Justin says "are you ready to meet your mother in law?" Kimberly looks back at him and smiles.

After spending over three hours catching up with his mother and her holding the babies and having lunch with Kimberly, Justin decided to ask his mother about her and Jason. "Jason is not speaking to me over a letter that surfaced from Shantelle, you know Jordan jr. wife?" Alex said. She couldn't tell him what the letter said without knowing he was going to ask her about Jordan sr. being in her life for all those years because he had asked her before. "So Shantelle gave him a letter stating what? What could she have over you Ma?" Justin asked. "She gave him a letter that told him that I am really his mother that Tricia wasn't his mother and that Jordan Sr. is his biological father and not Junnie." Alex tried to explain. Looking at his mother in utter discuss Justin says "How many more secrets are you hiding? I do believe that Jordan Sr. is all of our fathers for years I said that we all look just like his son Jordan jr. That man employed me and told me it was because he cared he has been sending me money ever since I got into the military. Keeping in touch with me I always thought something was up with that but never said anything. You are one of the most secretive women I know that has secrets that will spilt a whole nation. Funny is I'm not even mad with you mom I feel like you just were scared and didn't know how to tell us." "Baby boy it has been so many times that I have been wanting to tell you things but couldn't to protect Jordie. I have had so much going on in my mind trying to figure out how I was going to sit you all down and tell you all that it has been all a lie and now things have gotten out of hand and to just think that if it ever comes out that Anastasia is not you guys biological sister I will be so lost." Alexander explains to Justin. Thinking that she was going to get off so easy with her story since Justin was so calm, Alexander tried to talk to him like he was so stupid. "She is a mother-fucking liar!" Jason yells as he walks through the front door. This lady has made me believe for all these years that my mother was not only that junkie bitch she used to work for but that she was my fucking aunt only to find out that all of my life has been a fucking lie and I could have been out there fucking my own cousin or something. Her and that fucking Jordie are some sick individuals and I hate her Justin don't believe the hype." Jason yells as he walks through the kitchen door and hears what Alexander is tell Justin about why she kept the secrets for so long. "Mother I came back her to help because I received a letter that had paid for flights for me and my wife and a letter that stated that you would need me by your side my brother was dying. I guess that was a lie as well. What in the fuck is really going on? Why did you bring me back to this bull shit I have been away for over 22 years and I wasn't missing anything I fucking hated living with you when I had to and after finding all this out I'm going to go pay Jordan a visit and see if he knows anything about this." Justin said with tears coming down his face. Knowing that going to Jordan may not be the wise thing for him to do but Justin asked Jason to take him to their brother so that they could talk about all that has surfaced. In a panic Alexander screams, "PLEASE DON'T GO TO HIM HIS FATHER DON'T WANT HIM TO KNOW ANY OF THIS!!!". "Fuck him he dead now so what can he do to me?" Justin asked. "Jordie is not dead he is alive and well. "Alex says with tears coming down her face. "WHAT ARE YOU CRAZY!!!? That nigga is dead we went to the funeral." That was all a hokes he is alive he is alive he is alive. Alex just kept repeating her. "Would you just SHUT THE FUCK UP! Justin demanded. You are nothing but a complete liar I want nothing else to do with you at all, Come on Jason and Kim let's get out of here I can't stand another minute in this house with her." Justin demanded.

Acknowledgements

Without the love and support of the ones who believed in me I would have never stopped and wrote my book. I took a step that I never thought I would ever take and became the writer that has always been trapped inside of me. This is my very first book I hope you all enjoyed reading my part one of many. But first I need to say a few special thank you.

A great big shout out to Arminta McKinney who always pushes me even in silence she is my true MVP from every dream I shared with her she always made sure that I achieved them goal by goal. Checking in on me from time to time and allowing me to see my growth you Rock AM! To my four children- (Tiye'l, Leroy, Daniel, and Taylah) thank you for being my reason to push this book through everything you guys have been my purpose. To Octavia and Cody- My sister girls for telling me that day at the table that I could be a book writer look at me now working on novels and not just short stories and advice columns. To Renata- My biggest fan and critic she sat there and helped me word for word story line for story line. Helping me find ways to develop my characters. To Brittany- Thank you for believing that I could be your shining star and believing that in your words. "I'm the shit!" you rock Brittany. To my family, friends and co-workers- Thank you for being my guinea pigs and reading this novel and so many other short stories that I have created and giving me the inspiration to strive for more. Thank you for being my village and having my back when I ran out of ideas and asking me what was coming next probing me to move on with my story line. To my Jakiba I want to say thank you for telling me "Go for it! You can do it!"

Game of Lies:Hidden Truth

About the Author

Tiesha Davis

This is Tiesha Davis' first novel. A hard working mother of four teenagers and wife and a student Tiesha has found what her gift is with the stroke of a pen. Not knowing that writing was a hidden gift Tiesha picked up a pencil one day and since that day that she created Jordan and Shantelle, Tiesha's dreams have started to come true. One day Tiesha started writing from the heart creating her dreams with each stroke of the pencil. Tiesha will leave you on the edge of your seats with this erotic thriller. Stay tuned as the Author will draw you in with this plot and many more to come.